Isobel frowned. *Desertion* was such a damning word and, ironically, it contained more emotion than Constantin had ever revealed during the one year of the marriage that they had spent together.

Who was she kidding? When she pictured his hard, sculpted features it was impossible to believe he had a vulnerable side. Constantin did not *do* emotions. It was far more likely that the reason he had given for seeking a divorce had been coldly calculated. But she *would not* take all the blame for the failure of their marriage, Isobel thought fiercely. Constantin needed to realize that she was not a pushover like she had been when he had married her, and he *couldn't* have things all his way. Once, she had been overawed by him. But she was determined to end their marriage as his equal.

Chantelle Shaw lives on the Kent coast and thinks up her stories while walking on the beach. She has been married for over thirty years and has six children. Her love affair with reading and writing Harlequin romance novels began as a teenager, and her first book was published in 2006. She likes strong-willed, slightly unusual characters. Chantelle also loves gardening, walking and wine!

Chantelle Shaw

—

To Wear His Ring Again

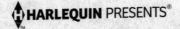

HARLEQUIN PRESENTS®

Recycling programs
for this product may
not exist in your area.

ISBN-13: 978-0-373-13315-4

To Wear His Ring Again

First North American Publication 2015

HARLEQUIN®

www.Harlequin.com

Printed in U.S.A.

To Wear His Ring Again

CHAPTER ONE

'THIS IS THE address you asked for. Grosvenor Square W1.' The taxi driver glanced over his shoulder at his passenger, who was still sitting on the back seat, puzzled that she hadn't climbed out of the car. 'Is this where you want to go, love? Or do you want me to take you somewhere else?'

Butterflies danced in Isobel's stomach as she stared out of the black cab, and for a moment she was tempted to ask the cabbie to drive on. The Georgian town house looked exactly the same as she remembered; the four storeys of mullioned windows gleamed in the spring sunshine, reflecting the trees in the park opposite. She had loved the house when she had lived there with Constantin, but now its elegant grandeur seemed to mock her.

She was surprised by how emotional she felt to return, two years after she had walked out of the front door for the last time and turned her back on her marriage. Perhaps she should just sign the divorce petition burning a hole in her handbag and post it back to Constantin's lawyer. What was the point in seeing him again after all this time and dredging up the past?

The truth was that she had never really known her husband. When they had met three years ago, she had been dazzled by his charm and seduced by his smouldering sexuality. At first, their relationship had been a roller coaster of sizzling passion, but after their wedding Constantin had changed into a remote stranger. With hindsight, she realised that she had never truly understood the enigmatic Italian who went by the exotic title of Marchese Constantin De Severino.

She visualised the legal document in her handbag with the heading in stark black typeface: *Affidavit in support of divorce—desertion*, and felt a rush of anger at the reason Constantin had given for seeking a divorce. It was true that she had been the one to leave the marriage, and so technically she supposed she *had* deserted him. But he had given her no option but to leave him. He had driven her away with his coldness and his uncompromising attitude towards her career.

She frowned. *Desertion* was such a damning word and, ironically, it contained more emotion than Constantin had ever revealed during the one year of the marriage that they had spent together.

Who was she kidding? When she pictured his hard, sculpted features it was impossible to believe he had a vulnerable side. Constantin did not *do* emotions. It was far more likely that the reason he had given for seeking a divorce had been coldly calculated. But she *would not* take all the blame for the failure of their marriage, Isobel thought fiercely. Constantin needed to realise that she was not a pushover as she had been when he had married her, and he *couldn't* have things all his way. Once, she had been overawed by him. But she was determined to end their marriage as his equal.

'This is fine, thanks,' she told the taxi driver as she stepped onto the pavement and leaned down to the cab window to pay the fare. The breeze lifted her honey-blonde hair from her shoulders.

Recognition dawned on the cabbie's face. 'I know who

you are! You're that singer Izzy Blake from the Stone Ladies. My daughter is a big fan.' He thrust a notepad into Isobel's hand. 'Can I be cheeky and ask for your autograph for my Lily?'

She took the pen he handed her and signed her name. Being recognised by the public was something Isobel doubted she would ever be entirely comfortable with, but she never forgot that the band owed their success to their many thousands of fans worldwide.

'Are you in London to give a concert?' the cabbie asked her.

'No, we finished our European tour in Berlin last week, but I think we're due to play in London in the autumn.' She had given up trying to remember the exact details of the band's hectic schedule. For the past two years, her life had been a blur of airport lounges and hotel lobbies in whichever town, state, continent where the band was performing. She tore a page out of the cabbie's notebook. 'Give me your email address and I'll make sure you're sent a couple of tickets so you can take your daughter to the Stone Ladies' next concert.'

The taxi driver thanked her, and when he drove away Isobel unconsciously clenched her fingers around the strap of her bag as she climbed the front steps of the house and rang the doorbell. Despite her determination to remain cool and calm, she could feel her heart thudding painfully hard beneath her ribs. She was not *nervous* at the prospect of seeing Constantin again, she assured herself. She thought of the divorce petition he had sent her, and the accusatory, condemning word *desertion* had the same effect on her temper as a red rag to a bull.

'Damn you, Constantin,' she muttered beneath her breath, just before the door was opened by a familiar figure.

'Madam,' Constantin's butler greeted her gravely, his

measured tone and imperturbable features revealing no hint of surprise at her sudden reappearance after two years.

'Hello, Whittaker. Is my...husband...at home?' She was annoyed by the huskiness in her voice as she stumbled over the word husband. He wouldn't be for much longer and she would be free to move on with her life.

She had read in a newspaper that Constantin was in London to attend the opening of a new De Severino Eccellenza store—more commonly known by the company's logo DSE—in Oxford Street, and she had planned her visit for Sunday morning because, even though he was a workaholic, it was unlikely that Constantin would have gone to the office on a Sunday.

'The Marquis is downstairs in the gymnasium.' The butler stepped back to allow her to enter the house. 'I will inform him on the internal phone that you are here.'

'No!' Isobel stopped him. She wanted to retain the element of surprise. As Whittaker's brow pleated in a faint frown she added quickly, 'He...he's expecting me.' It was the truth of sorts, she assured herself. No doubt Constantin was waiting for her to meekly sign the divorce petition, but he probably did not expect her to deliver the document in person. She hurried along the hall towards the stairs that led down to the basement.

Constantin had had the gym installed soon after their marriage so that he could work out at home rather than stop off at his private health club after he'd spent all day at the office. Descending the stairs, Isobel could hear a rhythmic pounding noise. The door to the gym was open, and she had a clear view of him slamming his fists into a punchbag. He was totally focused on what he was doing and did not notice her.

Her mouth ran dry as she stood in the corridor and studied him. She had forgotten how *big* he was! He owed his six-feet-plus height to his American mother, who—on one of the rare occasions when he had spoken about his family—Constantin had told Isobel had been a successful model before she had married his father.

She guessed his slashing cheekbones and classically sculpted features were also a result of his mother's genes, but in every other way he was pure Italian male, with exotic olive skin and dark, almost black, glossy hair that grew in luxuriant waves and refused to be completely tamed by the barber's scissors. His shorts and gym vest revealed his powerful thigh and shoulder muscles, and the curling black hairs on his chest were damp with sweat as he powered his fists into the punchbag.

He would need to take a shower after his punishing workout, Isobel mused. An unbidden memory slid into her mind of the early days of their marriage when she had often come down to the gym to watch Constantin work out, and afterwards they had shared a shower. The two years that they had been apart melted away as she remembered running her hands over his naked, muscular thighs and stretching her fingers around his powerful erection while he smoothed a bar of soap over her breasts and continued down her quivering, shivering body until she begged him to end the torment and take her hard and fast, leaning against the wall of the shower cubicle.

Dear heaven! Scalding heat swept through her veins, and she could not repress a choked sound in her throat that immediately alerted Constantin to her presence. His head shot round, and for perhaps thirty seconds Isobel saw a stunned expression on his face before his chiselled features hardened and became unreadable. He pulled off his boxing gloves and strolled towards her.

'Isabella!'

His deep voice was as sensuous as bittersweet chocolate, and his use of the Italian version of her name evoked a flood of molten desire in the pit of Isobel's stomach. How could he have such a devastating effect on her after all this time? Working in the music industry, she was often in the company of good-looking men, but she'd never felt a spark of desire for anyone she'd met. She had put her lack of interest down to the fact that she was still legally married—for although she and Constantin had parted on bad terms she believed in fidelity within marriage. But with a flash of near despair she realised that no other man excited her as her husband did. For the past two years her sexual desires had lain dormant, but one look at Constantin was all it had taken to arouse her body to a fever pitch of lustful longing.

Utterly thrown by her reaction to him, she felt an urge to turn and flee back up the stairs. But it was too late; he halted in front of her, standing unnervingly close so that she inhaled the sensual musk of his maleness.

Beads of sweat glistened on his skin. Isobel found herself wanting to run her fingers through the lock of sable hair that had fallen forwards onto his brow and trace the close-trimmed black stubble that shaded his jaw and upper lip. Every muscle in her body tautened defensively as she fought the effect he had on her. She was unaware that she reminded Constantin of a nervous colt who might bolt at any second.

'Don't hide in the shadows, *cara*,' he drawled. 'I don't know why you're here, but I assume you have a very good reason to let yourself into the house, two years after you ran away.'

His cynical tone hurtled Isobel back in time to the dying days of their marriage when they had been at constant loggerheads.

'I didn't run away,' she snapped.

His heavy black brows rose, but it was his eyes that held her spellbound. The first time Isobel had met him—when she had been a temporary secretary sent by the agency to work for the CEO at the London office of the exclusive jewellery and luxury goods company, De Severino Eccellenza—she had been mesmerised by Constantin's brilliant blue eyes that were such an unexpected contrast to his swarthy, Latin looks.

He shrugged. 'All right, you didn't run. You *sneaked* out while I was on a business trip. I came home to find your note informing me that you had gone on tour with the band and wouldn't be coming back.'

Isobel gritted her teeth. 'You knew I was going to go with the Stone Ladies—we had discussed it. I left because, if I hadn't, we would have destroyed each other. Don't you remember the row we had the morning before you went to France, or the argument we'd had the day before, or the day before that? I couldn't take it any more.' Her voice shook. 'We couldn't even be together in the same room without tension flaring. It was time to end our train wreck of a marriage.'

A throb of pain shot across her brow, causing her to draw a sharp breath and reminding her of the tension headaches she'd suffered during her marriage. She and Constantin were arguing already, mere moments after meeting each other again.

'Besides, I didn't let myself into the house,' she said in a carefully controlled voice. 'I left my door key with my wedding ring on your desk two years ago.' The symbolic gesture of pulling her gold wedding band from her finger had dealt the final devastating blow to her heart, Isobel remembered painfully. 'Whittaker let me in.' She opened her handbag and pulled out the divorce petition. 'I came to return this.'

Constantin flicked his eyes to the document. 'You must be in a desperate hurry to officially end our marriage, if you couldn't wait until tomorrow to put the paperwork in the post.'

Riled by his mocking tone, she opened her mouth to agree that she was impatient to sever the final links between them. She was wearing four-inch heels but Constantin towered over her and she had to tilt her head to meet his cobalt-blue gaze. It was an unwise move, she realised as her eyes dropped to his sensual, full-lipped mouth and her pulse quickened. Her tongue darted out to moisten her suddenly dry lips, and she glimpsed a dangerous glitter in his eyes as he followed the betraying gesture before he roamed his gaze over her in a leisurely inspection that made Isobel's skin tingle.

'You're looking good, *Isabella*,' he drawled.

Her stupid heart performed a somersault, but she managed to respond coolly, 'Thank you.' The old Isobel had struggled to accept compliments graciously, but maturity had given her the self-assurance to be able to look in a mirror and acknowledge that she was attractive.

That did not mean she hadn't spent ages debating what to wear for her meeting with Constantin. Her aim had been to look sophisticated yet give the impression that she hadn't tried too hard and she had eventually settled on dark blue jeans from her favourite designer, teamed with a plain white tee shirt and—for a confidence booster—a pillar-box-red jacket. She had left her long, layered hair loose, and wore minimum make-up—just mascara to emphasise her hazel eyes, and a slick of rose-coloured gloss on her lips.

She saw Constantin glance at her handbag. 'From the new De Severino Eccellenza collection,' he noted. 'Rather ironic, seeing that you always made a fuss when I gave you DSE items while we were together. When you bought your bag I hope you explained that you are my wife, and asked for a discount.'

'Of course I didn't,' Isobel said stiffly. 'I can afford to pay the full price.'

There seemed no point trying to explain that when they had been together she had felt guilty when Constantin had given her DSE jewellery and accessories because everything in the collection was incredibly expensive, and she hadn't wanted to seem like a gold-digger who had married him for his money.

In the last two years her successful singing career had earned her an income that was unbelievable to a girl who had grown up in an ex-colliery village in the north of England, where poverty and deprivation had sucked the life and soul out of the men who had been unemployed since the pit had closed a decade ago. She doubted Constantin would understand how good it made her feel to be able to pay for her own clothes and jewellery after the shame she'd felt as a teenager, knowing that her family relied on handouts from the state.

She glanced at his autocratic features and her heart sank. She had always been conscious of the social divide between them. Constantin was a member of the Italian aristocracy, a man of noble birth and incredible wealth and sophistication, and it was perhaps unsurprising that a miner's daughter had struggled to fit into his exclusive lifestyle. But she was no longer plagued by the insecurities of her youth. Her successful career had given her a sense of self-assurance and pride.

'I don't want to rake up the past,' she told him firmly.

His eyes narrowed appraisingly on her face, and she sensed he was surprised by her new confidence. 'What *do* you want?'

Isobel's intention had been to make it clear that she would not accept responsibility for the collapse of their marriage. But her fiery words were replaced by a different kind of fire in her belly as she watched him pick up a towel and rub it over his arms and shoulders. He pulled off his gym vest and dragged the towel across the whorls of sweat-damp dark hairs that grew thickly on his chest and arrowed down over his flat abdomen.

She jerked her eyes guiltily from where the fuzz of hairs disappeared beneath the waistband of his shorts, and clenched her hand to prevent herself from reaching out and skimming her fingers over his rock-hard abdominal muscles. She had often thought about him in the past two years, but her memory had not done him justice. He was so gorgeous he made her insides melt.

Her skin prickled as every nerve-ending on her body became acutely attuned to Constantin's raw sex appeal. Something primitive and purely instinctive stirred in the pit of her stomach. Her brain sensed that he represented danger, but the alarm bells ringing inside her head were obliterated by the sound of her blood thundering in her ears.

Silence quivered between them like an overstretched elastic band. Constantin frowned when she failed to respond to his question, but he glimpsed the unguarded expression in her eyes and his lips curled into a predatory smile.

'Ah, I think I understand, *cara*. Were you hoping we could get together for old times' sake, before we make our separation legal?'

'Get together?' For a moment Isobel didn't understand. She could not control the heat that surged through her when Constantin's gaze lingered on her breasts, and to her horror she felt her nipples harden and prayed he could not see their jutting points outlined beneath her clingy tee shirt.

'There were no problems with one aspect of our marriage,' he murmured. 'Our sex life was so explosive it was off the Richter scale.'

He was talking about *sex*! Her eyes clashed with his glittering gaze and her fingers itched to wipe the mockery from his face. 'You think I came here to...*proposition* you? In your dreams,' she told him furiously.

Her blood boiled. How dared Constantin suggest that the reason for her visit was because she wanted to sleep with him—*for old times' sake*? But her treacherous mind responded to his provocative suggestion and she visualised them naked and writhing on the gym mat, limbs entangled and their skin damp with sweat as he drove his body into hers in a relentless rhythm.

Heat scalded her cheeks, and she did not trust herself to say anything else to him that wouldn't result in them having one of the vicious arguments that had been a regular feature of the last months of their marriage. Dignified silence seemed her best strategy, but as she swung away from him his gravelly, accented voice stopped her from marching up the stairs.

'You have often been in my dreams these past two years, Isabella. The nights can be long and lonely...can't they?'

Could she possibly have heard regret in his voice? Was there any chance that he had missed her even half as much as she had missed him? Slowly, she turned back to face him, and immediately realised that she had indulged in wishful thinking. He was lounging in the doorway, bare-chested, beautiful and totally aware that he turned her on.

How could she have thought that Constantin might hide a vulnerable side beneath his arrogance? The idea that she had hurt him when she had left two years ago was laughable, Isobel thought bitterly. If he had a heart, he kept it locked behind a wall of impenetrable steel that nothing and no one could breach.

'I don't imagine you have spent many nights alone,' she said tautly, 'not if the stories in the tabloids linking you with numerous beautiful models and socialites are to be believed.'

He shrugged. 'There were occasions when it was necessary for me to invite women to social events—' he sent her a piercing glance '—since my wife wasn't around to accompany me. Unfortunately the gutter press thrive on scandal and intrigue, and if none exist they fabricate lies.'

'Are you saying that you didn't have affairs with those women?'

His mocking expression gave nothing away. 'If you're trying to lead me into admitting adultery as a reason for us to divorce—forget it,' he said coolly. 'You're the one who walked out of our marriage.'

Frustration surged through Isobel and she wanted to demand a straight answer from him. The idea that he had slept with the women he had been photographed with made her feel sick with jealousy. But as Constantin had pointed out, *she* had been the one to leave, and she had no right to ask him about his personal life. He was a red-blooded male with a high sex drive, and common sense told her that he was unlikely to have remained celibate for the past two years.

The adrenalin that had pumped through her veins when she had psyched herself up to see Constantin drained away, and she suddenly felt weary and strangely deflated. It had been a stupid idea to come here.

She looked down at the divorce petition in her hand and calmly ripped it in half.

'I want a divorce as much as you do, but for the reason that we have lived apart for more than two years. If you continue to state my desertion as a reason, I'll begin divorce proceedings against you, citing your unreasonable behaviour.'

He jerked his head back as if she had slapped him and his eyes glittered with anger. '*My* behaviour? What about how you behaved? You were hardly a devoted wife, were you, *cara*?' He made the endearment sound like an insult. 'In fact you went out with your friends so often that I almost forgot I had a wife.'

'I saw my friends because, for some reason that I have never understood, you had turned into the ice man. We were two strangers who happened to live in the same house. But I needed more, Constantin. I needed you...'

Isobel broke off as the hard gleam in Constantin's eyes told her she was wasting her breath. 'I refuse to take part in a slanging match,' she muttered. She gave a hollow laugh. 'It's a telling indictment of our marriage that we can't even agree on how we're going to end it.'

She swung away from him and marched up the stairs, her back ramrod-straight. Reaching the ground-floor level, she hurried towards the front door but was forced to halt as the butler finished speaking on the house phone and moved to stand in front of her.

Whittaker held open the door to the sitting room. 'The Marquis requested that you wait in here while he takes a shower, and he will join you shortly.'

She shook her head. 'No, I'm leaving.'

Whittaker's polite smile did not falter. 'Mr De Severino hopes that you will stay and continue the discussion you began a few minutes ago. Shall I bring you some tea, madam?'

Before she could argue, Isobel found that she had been

steered into the sitting room, and there was a faint click as Whittaker departed and shut the door behind him. She didn't understand what Constantin was playing at. It was clear they had nothing to discuss that could not be dealt with by their respective divorce lawyers. Her immediate thought was that she was not going to be a puppet controlled by the master puppeteer as had so often happened during their marriage.

She reached for the door handle just as the door opened and the butler entered carrying a tray with a silver teapot and a cafetière.

'I remembered that you prefer Earl Grey tea, madam,' he said, smiling as he held out a cup and saucer.

Good manners prevented Isobel from storming out of the house. She had always got on well with Whittaker, and her problems with her marriage were not the elderly butler's fault. Suppressing her irritation that Constantin had got his own way as he had so often done in the past, she wandered over to the window. The view of the park was familiar and evoked painful memories.

'I've just spoken to my lawyer and instructed him to send a new divorce petition for you to sign. You'll also have to give a written statement saying that we have lived apart for two years.'

At the sound of Constantin's clipped voice Isobel jolted and slopped tea into her saucer. She spun round, disconcerted to find him standing close to her. For such a big man he moved with the silent menace of a panther stalking its prey, she thought ruefully. The black jeans and polo shirt he had changed into emphasised his lethal good looks. His hair was still damp from his recent shower and the citrusy fragrance of soap mixed with his spicy cologne teased her senses.

'Giles still thinks I have good grounds to divorce you

for desertion.' Constantin's anger that she had thwarted him was evident in his harsh tone. 'But the legal advice is that it will be quicker to go with the fact that we have been separated for two years. The one thing we *can* both agree on is that we want a swift end to our marriage,' he drawled sardonically.

Determined to hide the pang of hurt that his words evoked, Isobel turned her gaze back to the window and stared once more at the pretty park at the centre of Grosvenor Square.

'When I was pregnant, I often used to stand here and imagine pushing our baby in a pram around the gardens,' she said softly. 'Our little girl would have been almost two and a half now.'

The shaft of pain in her chest was not as sharp as it had once been, but it was enough to make her catch her breath. Coming back to the house where she had lived when she had been pregnant had opened up the wound in her heart that would never completely heal. She had chosen one of the bedrooms at the back of the house for a nursery, and had been busy planning the colour scheme before she and Constantin had made that fateful trip to Italy.

She watched him pour himself a cup of coffee and felt a surge of anger that he had not reacted to the mention of their daughter. Nothing had changed, Isobel thought grimly. When she had lost their baby, twenty weeks into her pregnancy, she had been numb with grief. A few times she had tried to talk about the miscarriage with Constantin, but he had rebuffed her and become even more distant, and eventually she had stopped trying to reach him.

'Do you ever think about Arianna?' The nurse at the hospital had advised them to choose a name for their baby, even though she had been born too early to survive.

He sipped his coffee, and Isobel noted that he did not

meet her gaze. 'There's no point dwelling on the past,' he said shortly. 'Nothing can change what happened. All we can do is move forwards.'

Two years ago, she had been chilled by his lack of emotion, but as she looked closely at him and saw a nerve flicker in his cheek she realised that he was tenser than he appeared.

'Is that why you've begun divorce proceedings? You want to bury the past?'

He winced at her deliberate use of the word *bury*, and Isobel wondered if his mind pictured, as hers did, the small white marble tombstone in the grounds of the chapel at Casa Celeste—the De Severino family's historic home on the shores of Lake Albano—where they had laid Arianna to rest.

Constantin's eyes narrowed. 'Is there a point to this conversation? I haven't heard a word from you in two years. Why have you turned up out of the blue?'

He did not try to disguise his frustration. He had not anticipated this meeting with his soon-to-be ex-wife, and Constantin hated surprises. His shock when he had caught sight of Isobel standing in the doorway of the gym had sparked his anger that she had left him—even though he acknowledged that he had driven her away. She had a hell of a nerve to stroll back into the house, looking so beautiful that he'd been instantly and embarrassingly aroused.

His temper was not improved when he felt his hand shake as he lifted his cup to his lips and gulped down his coffee, scalding the back of his throat in the process. He did not want her here, stirring up memories of the past that he had successfully kept locked away. An image flashed into his mind of their tiny, perfectly formed baby girl who had never lived. Pain flared inside him, but he controlled it as he always did, by force of will, and blocked out the memories.

Harder to control was his body's reaction to Isobel. Unwanted memories were not the only thing she was stirring, Constantin acknowledged self-derisively as he shifted position in an effort to hide the bulge of his arousal. No other woman had ever turned him on as hard and fast as Isobel.

He remembered the first time he had met her. She had hurtled into his office half an hour late for work, a flurry of honey-blonde hair framing a strikingly beautiful face, and announced that she had been sent by the temp agency to cover for his office assistant who was on maternity leave. He'd cut short her explanation of why she was late, but his impatience had died when he had looked into her wide hazel eyes and felt a shaft of desire so strong that it had literally taken his breath away.

From that moment his sole aim had been to take her to bed, a feat he'd achieved within the month. Discovering that he was her first lover had elicited emotions he had not believed himself capable of. The weekend they had spent together in Rome had been the best—and worst— of his life.

It had been the beginning of the nightmares that had haunted him ever since he'd woken in the middle of the night, sweating and shaking, and utterly appalled by the truth that his dream had revealed. He had looked at Isobel sleeping innocently beside him, and realised that for her safety he could not allow their relationship to continue.

CHAPTER TWO

THE SUN GLINTING through the windows turned Isobel's hair to spun gold. A sensation he could not define tugged in Constantin's chest, but he ignored it and forced himself to study her objectively.

Her clothes bore the hallmarks of superb design; the close-fitting jeans drew his attention to her endlessly long legs and her tee shirt snugly moulded her firm breasts. A gold chain around her neck was her only item of jewellery. His mouth thinned as he glanced at her bare left hand and pictured her wedding ring and diamond engagement ring that she had left behind when she had abandoned their marriage to pursue her career.

Her physical appearance had changed little in two years. Her face, with its high cheekbones and firm jaw that gave a clue to her determined character, was as beautiful as he remembered, and her hazel eyes fringed with long lashes were clear and intelligent. Her natural blonde hair was sexily tousled, and the just-got-out-of-bed style made him want to run his fingers through the silky layers.

His eyes sought hers, and he was intrigued when she met his gaze with calm self-assurance where once she would have blushed and looked away. There was something very alluring about a woman who was comfortable in her own skin and Constantin felt an ache of desire in his groin, but, perversely he was irritated by the self-confidence that she had developed after she had left him.

'I'm not the only one of us to have featured in the press,' he said abruptly. 'The Stone Ladies' success has been meteoric and the band has won a raft of music awards. How does it feel to be a famous star?'

Isobel shrugged. 'Frankly, it seems unreal. In two years the band has gone from playing small gigs in pubs to performing in huge arenas in front of thousands of people. Success is amazing, of course, but if I'm honest I find the media interest in my private life hard to deal with.'

'Particularly as the paparazzi are fascinated by your relationship with one of the male band members,' Constantin said sardonically. 'I'm guessing the record company want the band's image to be squeaky clean for your teenage fans, which is why your profile on social media sites makes no mention of the fact that you are married.'

Isobel sighed, sensing that they were heading towards an old argument. 'I've explained that Ryan is just a friend. I'm close to everyone in the band. We grew up together and Ben, Carly and Ryan are like my family. You never understood how important they are to me and I know you resented my friendships, but the truth was that the more you pushed me away, the more I needed to be with people who cared about me, people I could trust.'

Constantin frowned. 'I never gave you any reason not to trust me.'

'I don't mean I suspected you of seeing other women behind my back.' In a way, if he had been unfaithful it would have been easier to understand, Isobel thought painfully. She would have been hurt, but she would have accepted that she'd made a mistake by marrying a notorious playboy, and eventually she would have got over him.

She stared at his handsome face and her heart clenched.

She had written songs about falling in love at first sight but she'd never really believed it could happen—until she'd met Constantin.

When she had hurried into his office on her first day at her new job, her eyes had crashed with his cobalt-blue gaze, and the world had tilted on its axis. She had expected the CEO of a world-famous company to be older, possibly with thinning hair and a thickening waistline, but Constantin was a superb example of masculine perfection, with exotic film-star looks and the commanding presence of a world leader. She had felt intimidated by his height and powerful build, by his smouldering sensuality that made her acutely aware of her femininity. But then he had smiled and she had felt a yearning ache in the pit of her stomach that she had instinctively known only he could assuage.

Constantin put his coffee cup on the tray, and his eyes narrowed on Isobel's flushed face as he wondered what thoughts she was trying to hide behind the sweep of her long eyelashes. She looked amazing, he acknowledged. Following the miscarriage she had barely eaten and had lost weight dramatically, but now her slim figure was firm and toned. Did she have a lover? The thought oozed its poison into his head. She was a beautiful, sensual woman, and it was difficult to believe she had lived like a nun for the past two years.

He had seen her photograph on posters advertising the Stone Ladies' new album. There were pictures of her on giant billboards around London wearing a skirt that was barely more than a wide belt, which showed off her lissom thighs. She was a pin-up girl, a male fantasy, but he had no need of fantasies when he had X-rated memories of making love to her.

Those memories crowded his mind and his arousal became a potent, throbbing force. The atmosphere in the sitting room altered subtly. He heard the quickening sound of his breathing, or was it Isobel's? He looked into her eyes and watched them darken as her pupils dilated, and he knew she was remembering the white-hot hunger that had consumed them in the past and was simmering between them now.

Goosebumps prickled on the back of Isobel's neck when she saw the hard glitter in Constantin's eyes. The realisation that he still desired her filled her with panic and undeniable excitement. She tore her gaze from him and stared desperately at the empty teacup and saucer in her hand, suddenly realising that she was gripping the delicate bone china so tightly it was in danger of breaking. She took a step towards the coffee table, intending to put the cup and saucer on the tray, but her heel caught on the edge of the rug and she stumbled. Immediately two strong arms caught her, and when she regained her balance she found herself standing so close to Constantin that the tips of her breasts grazed his chest.

'Thanks.' She groaned inwardly when her voice emerged as a husky whisper. Her throat felt dry and her senses were swamped by the evocative scent of the spicy aftershave that he always wore. Her common sense told her to move away from him but she seemed to have lost control of her limbs as her mind flew back to the first time he had kissed her.

He had given her a lift home from work. Sitting next to him in his sleek sports car, she had felt even more overwhelmed by him than she did at the office. Her position as an assistant to his PA meant that her conversations with him had been mainly work related, and she had assumed that he barely noticed her. His request as they drove across the city for her to tell him about herself had thrown her into a panic, but he was her boss so she had obediently related the unexciting details of her life growing up in a small Derbyshire village.

When he had finally parked outside her flat, he'd turned to her, and his smile had made her heart skip a beat. 'You're very sweet,' he'd murmured.

His words had rankled. She hadn't wanted him to think she was a *sweet,* silly girl; she'd wanted him to think of her as a woman. Perhaps her feelings had shown in her eyes, because he had given a faint sigh before he'd lowered his head and covered her mouth with his.

Her body had come alive instantly. It was as if he had pressed a switch and awoken her sensuality that had been untested until that moment. Constantin had kissed her as she had imagined a man would kiss a woman, as she had dreamed of being kissed. She had been intoxicated by his mastery, and responded to his passionate demands with a fervency that had made him groan.

'Very soon I will make you mine, Isabella,' he'd warned her softly.

'How soon?' she'd replied, not caring that her eagerness revealed her lack of sophistication.

Now Isobel was three years older, but she was trapped by Constantin's sexual magnetism and felt as though she had flown back in time to when she had been a shy junior secretary who had been kissed senseless by the most exciting man she had ever met. Her heart jerked against her ribs as she watched his head descend, but her stomach plummeted with disappointment when he halted with his lips centimetres from hers.

'Why did you walk out on me?' he said harshly. 'You didn't even have the decency to tell me to my face that you were clearing out. All I got was an insultingly brief note to say that *you* had decided we should end our marriage.'

Isobel swallowed. It was impossible to think properly

when his lips were tantalisingly close, and even more impossible to believe that she had heard a note of hurt in his voice. She longed to close the gap between them, to slide her hand into the silky dark hair at his nape and urge his mouth down on hers. It took all her will power to step away from him.

'Why did you marry me?' She countered his question with one of her own. 'I've often wondered. Was it only because I was pregnant with your child? I believed our relationship was based on more than sexual attraction, but after I had the miscarriage you were so distant. I couldn't get close to you, and you never wanted to talk about... about what had happened. Your coldness seemed to indicate that you wished I wasn't your wife.'

Constantin had always been able to read the emotions on Isobel's expressive features and the pain reflected in her hazel eyes caused him a pang of guilt. He knew he had not given her the support she had needed when she'd lost the baby. He'd been unable to talk about it, and had dealt with his emotions the way he always did, by burying them deep inside and concentrating on running a global business empire. He could hardly blame her for turning to her friends, but he had felt jealous of her closeness to the other members of the band, and in particular her obvious affection for the guitarist, Ryan Fellows.

The cover of the Stone Ladies' new album was an arty black and white picture of the two most photogenic band members—Isobel and Fellows—riding a unicorn. No doubt the romantic image would appeal to the band's thousands of fans, but when Constantin had seen the album cover he'd felt an overwhelming desire to rearrange the guitarist's pretty-boy features with his fist.

The idea that Isobel and Fellows might be lovers evoked a corrosive acid burn in his gut. Isobel had accused him of resenting her friends, and he acknowledged it was the truth. He had been unable to control his possessive feelings, which in turn had made him afraid that he had inherited his father's dangerous jealousy.

He looked at her tense face. It must have taken a lot of guts for her to have come back to the house that he knew held poignant memories for her. He thought of the mural of farm animals that she had been painting on the walls of the nursery. The mural was unfinished and the room was empty. He'd sent the cot and nursery equipment back to the shop and never went into the room that had been destined for their daughter.

The miscarriage had broken Isobel, and it was a measure of her strength of will that she had recovered to be this beautiful, self-assured woman—although close scrutiny revealed faint shadows in her eyes that Constantin guessed would never completely fade. One thing was certain. She deserved his honesty.

'Three years ago we were lovers briefly. The weekend we spent at my apartment in Rome was fun, but...' he shrugged '...I had no desire for a prolonged relationship—and I thought you understood that.' When he had ended the affair shortly after they had returned to London he had assured himself it was for the best to call a halt before things got out of hand. Isobel had needed to understand that the words long-term and commitment were not in his vocabulary.

He exhaled heavily. 'But then fate dealt an unexpected card. When you told me you were pregnant you must have realised that I would not allow my child to be born illegitimate. Marriage was the only option. I could not neglect my duty to my child or to you.'

Isobel flinched. *Duty* was an ugly little word. The realisation that Constantin had proposed marriage because he had felt responsible for her evoked a bitter taste in her mouth. She had told Constantin she was pregnant with his baby because she'd believed he had the right to know. She had been stunned when he'd asked her to marry him. After all, it was the twenty-first century, and being a single mother was no longer regarded as unusual or shameful. When he had proposed, she had convinced herself that he must have some feelings for her. But the stark truth was that she had seen what she had wanted to see.

Yet her stubborn nature still refused to give up the idea that they had shared something meaningful. 'We had some good times in the beginning,' she reminded him.

'I don't deny it. We were going to be parents, and for our child's sake it was important to build an amicable relationship with each other, additional to our sexual compatibility.'

Isobel swallowed the golf ball that had become lodged in her throat. Had Constantin simply been building an *amicable* relationship with her when he had filled the house with yellow roses after she had mentioned that they were her favourite flower? Had she imagined the closeness between them that had grown stronger every day of their three-week honeymoon in the Seychelles?

She stared at his chiselled features and wondered why she had ever believed she had seen warmth in his eyes that glittered as hard and bright as sapphires. What a fool she had been. Despite everything that happened, his coldness to her in the last months of their marriage, deep down she had believed there was a chance that they might one day get back together. That fragile sense of hope had now gone and she was shocked by how badly it hurt.

She turned her head towards the window. The sun streaming through the glass was so bright, and surely it was the glare that was making her eyes water? As if she were looking through a kaleidoscope, she saw the fractured images of a woman pushing a pram through the park with a tall, handsome man at her side. But when she blinked, the vision disappeared, just as her dreams had done.

Somehow she marshalled her thoughts and emotions, and even managed a cool smile when she looked back at Constantin.

'In that case there's nothing more to be said. I'll wait to receive a new divorce petition from your solicitor, which I will sign and return immediately. I understand that the legal proceedings are straightforward in an uncontested divorce.'

'I've instructed my lawyer to offer you a financial settlement.' Constantin frowned when she shook her head. 'I don't understand why you insisted on signing a prenuptial agreement that awarded you absolutely nothing.'

'Because I want nothing from you,' Isobel told him fiercely. 'I'm lucky to be able to earn a high income, but even if the band hadn't become successful I wouldn't have accepted a handout from you.'

Impatience glittered in his eyes. 'I see you've lost none of your prickly independence. You're the only woman I've ever known who got annoyed if I bought you presents.'

She hadn't wanted expensive gifts. What she had wanted he had been unable or unwilling to give her—love, his heart in exchange for hers, a marriage that was a true partnership. Did such a thing even exist? She'd seen little evidence of it in her parents' marriage, Isobel thought wryly. Perhaps her father had been right during one of their many rows about her doing homework rather than writing songs, when he had accused her of wasting her time chasing rainbows. Maybe happy-ever-after only happened in fairy tales.

Of their own volition her eyes fixed on Constantin's

face as she committed his sculpted features to her memory. The faintly cynical curve of his lips evoked a visceral ache in her belly.

She had to get out of the house *now*, before her wafer-thin composure cracked. Never had she been more thankful for the illusion of supreme confidence that performing with the band had given her. She walked unhurriedly across the room and glanced back at Constantin from the doorway. 'I'll instruct my lawyer to reject any financial offer from you.'

'Per l'amor di Dio!' He swore beneath his breath as he crossed the room with long strides. 'Dammit, Isobel, you are entitled to receive a settlement from me. The music industry can be fickle, and, although the band is riding high at the moment, no one can say what the future holds.'

Wasn't that the truth? Isobel thought emotively as the image of her tiny baby daughter flashed into her mind. Coming back to the house where she had dreamed of living as a happy family with Constantin and their child, she felt as though a protective layer had been scraped away from the scar tissue surrounding her heart.

'There's no reason any more for you to feel responsible for me,' she said tautly.

Her eyes clashed with his, and something in his brilliant blue gaze sent a warning signal to her brain. She sensed that he was mentally stripping her naked, and she was furious with her treacherous body as heat stole through her veins. He had always had the ability to decimate her equilibrium with one killer glance.

The sound of her phone ringing from the depths of her handbag was a welcome distraction. She retrieved the phone and glanced at the caller display before shooting an apologetic glance at Constantin. 'Do you mind if I answer this? It's Carly, probably calling to remind me that we'd arranged a shopping trip this afternoon.'

Her friend's cheerful voice greeted her. 'The photographer from *Rock Style* magazine wants to do the shoot tomorrow instead of midweek. Does that suit you? Okay, I'll let him know,' Carly said when Isobel confirmed she was free the next day. She cut the call and was about to drop her phone into her bag when it rang again. Assuming it was Carly with a second message, she lifted the phone to her ear and her heart jumped when a frighteningly familiar voice spoke.

'Hello, Izzy. It's David, your darling. Remember you wrote "To my darling David" when you gave me your autograph? I know you are in London and I hoped we could have dinner together.'

'How did you get my mobile number?' The instant Isobel blurted out the question she cursed herself. The police had advised her to stay calm and not reveal any emotion or engage in conversation with the man who had been stalking her for the past two months, but hearing David's voice filled her with panic. Her eyes jerked to the window and she scanned the pavement outside. Did he know her exact location in London? Her common sense told her it was unlikely that he had followed her here. But how on earth had he got hold of her mobile-phone number?

Without saying another word she cut the call and then checked the number of the last caller. The number had been withheld. She switched off her phone and dropped it into her handbag as if she feared it were an explosive device.

'What was that about?'

She met Constantin's curious gaze, unaware of the unease reflected in her eyes.

'Nothing.' Her response was automatic. There was no reason to involve Constantin. She would make a note of the call and file it with the other nuisance calls she had received from David as the police had advised her to do. More importantly, she would contact her network provider and change her mobile-phone number.

Constantin frowned. 'Your reaction suggested it was more than *nothing*. When you answered the call, you looked worried.' He placed his hand on Isobel's arm to prevent her from sidling out of the door. 'Do you have a problem with whoever called you?'

'No—it was just someone playing a joke.' She quickly thought up the excuse. Her problem right now was the way her body was reacting to Constantin's nearness. Her heart was racing and she could feel the pulse at the base of her throat beating erratically. She fought a crazy temptation to tell him about David—a fan who had developed an unhealthy obsession with her. The police were aware of the situation and everything was under control, she reassured herself. There was no point in involving her soon-to-be ex-husband.

In a matter of weeks she and Constantin would be divorced and it was likely that she would never see him again. The knowledge felt like a knife-blade through her heart. She pulled her arm free and stumbled into the hall. Her stiletto heels sounded like staccato gunfire on the marble floor as she half ran towards the front door.

'Goodbye, Constantin.' She could not resist one final glance over her shoulder at him. 'I hope one day you'll meet someone who can give you whatever it is you're looking for.'

'The role of Chairman of DSE has historically always passed to the eldest son of the next generation of the family. *It is my birthright, dammit!*'

Constantin paced around his uncle's office at the Rome

headquarters of DSE, his body taut with suppressed fury like a caged tiger enraged by its captivity. His eyes glittered as he stared at Alonso sitting calmly behind his desk. 'If I had been a year older when my father died I would have become Chairman a decade ago, but because I was seventeen, company rules dictated that the chairmanship must go to the next De Severino male who was of age— in this case, *you*, my father's brother. But now you wish to retire, and the chairmanship should revert to me. I intend to combine the role of Chairman with that of CEO, as my father did.'

Alonso cleared his throat. 'It is the belief among many members of the board that the two roles should be separated. An independent board chairman can better protect shareholder interests, leaving the CEO free to concentrate on running the business—which you do extremely well, Constantin.'

'Profits have risen year on year since I became CEO, but many times I have felt that I am working against the board rather than with their backing.' Constantin could barely contain his frustration. 'It is crucial for our continuing success that DSE takes advantage of emerging markets in Asia and South America. The board are slow to embrace change, but we must move fast to keep ahead of our competitors.'

'There is a concern that in your rush to take the company forwards, you have forgotten the standards and moral ethics of DSE that have been the backbone of the company since it was established by your great-grandfather nearly a century ago.'

Constantin slammed his hands down on his uncle's desk. 'I have forgotten nothing. I have lived and breathed DSE since I was a small boy, in the expectation that I would one day be fully responsible for the company. In what way have I forgotten the company's moral ethics?'

Instead of replying, Alonso looked pointedly at a copy of a popular gossip magazine lying on his desk. The front cover carried a photo of his nephew and an Italian glamour model, Lia Gerodi, emerging from a casino. From the amount of naked flesh on display, Miss Gerodi appeared to be experiencing a wardrobe malfunction, Alonso noted cynically.

Constantin shrugged as he glanced at the picture that had been taken a week ago. The only reason he remembered that particular evening was because it had been the night he had returned to Rome from London after his unexpected visit from Isobel. He had been in a foul mood, he recalled. The image of her walking out of the house in Grosvenor Square and climbing into a taxi, without once looking back, had been stuck in his mind. He'd felt churned up inside and, unusually for him, unable to rationalise his thoughts.

Lia had been phoning him for weeks, ever since they had met at a social event the details of which he did not remember. When he'd received a call from her as his jet had landed in Rome he had agreed to have dinner with her purely to take his mind off Isobel. The trip to the casino had been Lia's idea, and he suspected that she had tipped off the paparazzi, knowing that a picture of her with one of Italy's wealthiest businessmen would give her valuable media exposure that might boost her modelling career.

'This is not the image of the company that the board wishes to see advertised around the world,' Alonso said, tapping the photo with his forefinger. 'The public's perception of DSE must be of a company that delivers excellence, reliability and honesty. But how can the public trust that the company believes in those values, when the CEO, despite being married, leads a playboy lifestyle?'

'My private life has no bearing on my ability to run DSE,' Constantin growled. 'Shareholders are only interested in profits, not in my personal affairs.'

'Unfortunately that is not true, especially as you seem to have so many affairs.'

'You know how the press like to exaggerate.' Constantin's jaw clenched. 'If you are seriously considering not appointing me Chairman, who else do you have in mind?'

'My sister's son, Maurio. Since I have no son of my own,' Alonso continued when it became evident that Constantin was too stunned to comment, 'I have taken great interest in your younger cousin. I believe Maurio has many qualities that make him suitable for the role of Chairman, not least the fact that he is a happily married family man who is never likely to be photographed staggering out of a casino, clutching a bottle of Scotch in one hand and a half-naked bimbo in the other.'

'Maurio is spineless. He would be completely out of his depth as Chairman,' Constantin said harshly.

He swung away to stare out of the window while he fought the temptation to shake some sense into his uncle. *He* was the best person to take on the combined role of CEO and Chairman. It was what he had been born to do.

DSE was more than a business; it was his life, his identity. After he had witnessed the deaths of his father and stepmother when he was seventeen, Constantin had focused exclusively on the company as a way of preventing himself from thinking about the shocking tragedy. For ten years he had planned for the day when he took absolute control of DSE, but now there was a real danger that his destiny was going to be snatched away from him.

The hell it was, he thought grimly. DSE was his, and

he was *not* going to lose it. He turned back to his uncle. 'So, if the only problem you and the board have is with my image, I'll change it. I'll become a recluse. I'll live the life of a hermit if that's what it takes for you to choose me as your successor.'

Alonso looked at him steadily. 'I don't expect anything quite so drastic, Constantin. I simply ask that details of your love life are not a matter of media curiosity and titivation. I suggest that you resume your marriage. Prove that you can uphold the personal commitment you made when you married, and you may convince me that I can entrust complete control of DSE to you rather than your cousin.'

Constantin's eyes narrowed. 'That sounds like blackmail.'

His uncle's gaze did not falter. 'I don't care what it sounds like. The responsibility of appointing the next chairman is mine and mine alone, and unless I see you change your lifestyle to reflect the core values of DSE, I cannot be certain you are the right man for the job.'

CHAPTER THREE

It was a pity, Constantin thought bitterly later that night as he let himself into the house in Grosvenor Square, that the conversation with his uncle had not taken place a week ago, before he had made it clear to Isobel that their marriage was over.

It was past midnight and Whittaker had retired for the night, but the butler had left a decanter of malt whisky on the table in the sitting room with a note informing him that there were sandwiches in the fridge. Constantin had not eaten since lunch, but it had been a hell of a day, with meetings in Milan, Paris and London, and he had no appetite for food. He poured himself a large drink, sank down onto the sofa and picked up the television remote to flick through the channels.

How could Alonso consider handing the chairmanship of DSE to Maurio? His cousin was a pleasant enough young man, but he wouldn't last five minutes in the cut-throat corporate world. Constantin took a long swig of whisky and savoured its subtle warmth at the back of his throat. Nerve, daring and vision were the qualities required to head the billion-pound business that DSE had grown to be since *he* had become CEO. He had great plans for the future development of the company, but if his cousin was made Chairman, certain board members who were set in their ways would undoubtedly try to influence Maurio against him.

He took another gulp of whisky, and it occurred to him that maybe he drank too much. He shrugged. Alcohol worked well as an anaesthetic when he needed to blank out painful memories. If he drank enough, he might be able to snatch a few hours' sleep. Ever since Isobel's visit a week ago, his old nightmares had returned to haunt him and remind him of why he could not risk being with her.

He frowned as he recalled her strange reaction to the phone call she had received as she had been about to walk out of the door. He had not imagined the fearful expression in her eyes, although when he had asked her about the call she had denied anything was wrong. Beneath her air of self-confidence he had seen her vulnerability that had reminded him of the shy young secretary who used to watch him with her big, hazel eyes when she thought he was not aware of her.

He swore, and swallowed the rest of his drink before refilling his glass. He accepted that he bore most of the responsibility for the disintegration of their marriage, but Isobel was not completely blameless. He had lost count of the times he had come home from work to an empty house, and spent the evening alone while she had been singing with her band in pubs and clubs. Isobel had accused him of not understanding how important music was to her, and if he was honest he *had* resented the fact that the Stone Ladies had become an increasingly big part of her life.

When she had left him two years ago, he'd told himself it was best for both of them. Isobel had gone on to establish a hugely successful career. But now *his* career was under threat and the only way he could secure his rightful position as undisputed head of DSE was to persuade her to come back to him, days after he had admitted that the only reason he had married her was because she had been pregnant with his child. The irony of the situation was not lost on him. The expression that he had 'burned his bridges' could not be more apt, Constantin thought sardonically.

The wildlife documentary on the television failed to hold his interest. He flicked over the channel to a popular chat show and his attention was suddenly riveted on the screen.

'The Stone Ladies are arguably the most successful British folk-rock band of the past five years,' the chat-show host said. He went on to list the band's numerous music awards, but Constantin was only half listening as he stared at the image of Isobel that filled his TV screen. She was wearing a black leather minidress and thigh-high boots that drew attention to her endlessly long legs. Her blonde hair spilled over her shoulders and her lovely face was animated as she charmed the chat-show host with her quick wit and impressive self-assurance.

It was hard to believe that she was the same Isobel who had been painfully shy and overawed when he had invited her to spend the weekend with him at his penthouse apartment in Rome, Constantin brooded. He had patiently drawn her out of her shell, but he had still been shocked on their first night together when he had discovered that she was a virgin. His gut clenched as memories flooded his mind. What she had lacked in experience she had more than made up for in her eagerness to please him, he remembered.

On the television, the chat-show host had turned the interview with the band to questions about their personal lives. 'Ben and Carly, you announced your engagement a few months ago, and I believe you are planning your wedding for later this year?'

The couple, who were the drummer and keyboard

player, confirmed that they were planning to marry in the autumn. The interviewer then turned to Isobel and the fourth member of the band, Ryan Fellows. 'And how about you two?' the chat-show host asked coyly. 'You have never confirmed or denied the rumours that you are more than good friends. So, what is the exact nature of your relationship?'

Constantin gritted his teeth as he watched the long-haired guitarist put his arm around Isobel's shoulders. 'It's true that Izzy and I are *very* good friends.' Fellows grinned at Isobel and she smiled back at him. 'I may be making an announcement in the near future,' the guitarist added.

What did the blasted pretty-boy rock star mean by that? Anger boiled Constantin's blood as it occurred to him that the reason Isobel had insisted he could not cite her desertion as a reason for their divorce might be because she did not want to look bad to her fans when she went public about her relationship with Ryan Fellows.

Santa Madre! It was clear she had already got another man lined up to take *his* place. She had insisted that her relationship with Fellows was an innocent friendship, but as Constantin watched Isobel and the guitarist on the TV the closeness between the golden couple was evident for the world to see. Bile rose in his throat. How dared she flaunt her lover in public when she was still married to him? When they had married three years ago, their low-key wedding had gone unnoticed by the press. *But, hell, he felt like a cuckold.*

Constantin reached for the whisky bottle and filled his glass once more, while his mind worked furiously. If Isobel was involved with Ryan Fellows, why had she looked at *him* with a hunger in her eyes that had tempted him to bend her over the arm of the sofa and pull her jeans down so that he could give them both the satisfaction they craved? Could it be that the pretty-boy guitarist did not satisfy her?

His wife was a highly sensual woman, Constantin brooded. *Dio!* The scorching sexual chemistry between him and Isobel had been beyond anything he'd ever experienced with any other woman. When they had first been married they had spent hours indulging in erotic and highly satisfying lovemaking.

Did Isobel miss those wildly passionate sessions? When she had surprised him in the gym the other night, the sexual chemistry between them had been tangible. He had come so close to tumbling her down onto the gym mat and taking her hard and fast—and she would not have stopped him. She had pretended to be outraged, and had denied that she wanted him, but her body language had betrayed her.

Constantin's thoughts turned to his uncle's threat to deny him the chairmanship of DSE. When he had stormed out of Alonso's office it had not entered his mind to comply with the old man's ultimatum to resume his marriage in order to secure the position of Chairman. But as he stared at the TV screen and watched Isobel rest her hand on Ryan Fellows's thigh as they sat close together on the sofa, the burning rage inside him grew cold and congealed into a hard knot of fury.

DSE was his birthright. The company was the only thing that made him feel proud of being a De Severino. What was he otherwise? He was the son of a monster, taunted a voice inside his head. He dared not look too deeply inside himself for fear of what he might discover. He could not risk having a relationship that involved his emotions. DSE was his all-consuming mistress, his raison d'être, and he would do whatever it took to claim what was rightfully his.

By walking out on him two years ago, Isobel had

jeopardised his chance of becoming Chairman of DSE. But if he could persuade her to return to him, his uncle would appoint him Chairman—and once his position as head of the company was unchallengeable he would have no more need of his beautiful, fickle wife.

'Come in.' Isobel turned away from the mirror when she heard a knock on the door of the hotel room that she had been allocated as a dressing room.

'Wow,' Ryan said when he saw her, 'you look stunning.'

'You don't think the dress is over the top?' She gave another doubtful glance in the mirror at the gold sequined evening gown that hugged her body like a second skin and left one shoulder bare.

'The Duke of Beaufort's charity dinner is one of the most prestigious events in London's social calendar, and everything about tonight is going to be over the top. You look perfect for the occasion,' Ryan assured her.

'I can't believe the Stone Ladies have been asked to perform tonight.' She threw Ryan a wry smile. 'Did you ever imagine when we were playing gigs in pubs that we would one day be top billing at a grand party held in a five-star hotel?'

He laughed. 'It's crazy how fast things have happened. Sometimes I'm scared I'll wake up and find I'm back in Derbyshire working behind the bar of the ex-miners' social club.' Ryan hesitated. 'I reckon your dad would be proud of you, Izzy,' he said softly.

Her smile faded. 'I doubt it.'

Isobel recalled the conversation she'd had with her mother when they had stood at her father's graveside on the day of his funeral three months ago. Ann Blake had sobbed quietly, but Isobel had found it impossible to cry for her father, whose dour moods and abrasive temper had cast a shadow on her childhood so that she had tried to avoid him as much as possible when she had lived at home.

'Your father was a good man,' her mother had said suddenly. Catching Isobel's look of surprise, she had continued, 'I know he wasn't always easy to live with, especially when he was in one of his black moods, but he wasn't always like that. When I married him he was fun to be with and he had such hopes for us and for the future. But he changed after he had his accident, and he was no longer the strong, fit man he had been. When the coal mine closed and he couldn't find work it destroyed his pride, and losing his dream of making a better life for his family crushed his spirit.'

'It seemed as though he was determined to crush my spirit and my dreams of a different life,' Isobel had said fiercely. 'I know Dad often made you unhappy. I used to hear you crying in the kitchen when you thought I was in bed. I never understood why you stayed with him.'

'Part of him died with your brother. He never got over losing Simon—and he needed me. I took my marriage vows seriously—for better, for worse, for richer, for poorer, in sickness and in health.' Her mother had looked at Isobel curiously. 'You made the same vows when you married Constantin. You've never explained why your marriage ended. It's not my place to pry into your private life, but I can't help wondering if you gave up too soon. A year isn't a long time, and marriage isn't all hearts and flowers. You have to work at a relationship and make compromises to hopefully gain a better understanding of each other.'

She *had* tried to understand Constantin, Isobel thought grimly. But she need not have bothered, because she'd now had her darkest suspicions confirmed: that he had only married her because she had conceived his child. She had never told her mother about Arianna. It would have been cruel to tell Ann that she had lost a granddaughter as well as a son and husband.

Isobel dragged her thoughts back to the present when she realised that Ryan was speaking. 'I would never have met Emily if I'd stayed in Eckerton village, that's for sure.' He ran a hand through his fair hair, and said awkwardly, 'Izzy, I've done it. I've asked Emily to marry me—and she said yes.'

'Thank heavens for that,' Isobel said in a heartfelt voice as she flung her arms around Ryan's neck. 'You two were made for each other and I know you're going to be very happy together.'

Ryan's expression clouded. 'Emily makes me the happiest man in the world, but I don't deserve to feel like this. I keep thinking about Simon, and how he never had the chance to grow up and fall in love. If only I'd stopped him going into the reservoir that day.'

'Don't.' Isobel pictured her brother's mischievous grin. She could not imagine him as an adult. For her, Simon would always be fourteen, always laughing and fooling around. 'You know what a daredevil Simon was. He wouldn't have listened to you. I know you did everything you could to try and save him, and you have to stop blaming yourself.' She squeezed Ryan's arm. 'You and my brother were best friends. He would be glad that you're going to marry the woman you love.'

Ryan nodded slowly. 'I guess you're right. Thanks, Izzy.' He glanced at the clock. 'Hey, we'd better get moving. We're due on stage in ten minutes. How do you feel?'

'Nervous,' Isobel admitted. 'I always am before a performance, but I'll be fine once I start singing.' She was about to follow Ryan out of the room when her phone rang, and she walked back over to the dressing table where she had left it. Because she was in a hurry, she unthinkingly answered it without checking the identity of the caller, and she tensed when a familiar voice spoke.

'I'll be watching you tonight, Izzy. It is written in the stars that we are destined to be together for ever.'

She cut the call and the phone slid out of her trembling fingers. Was David here at the hotel? Could he be a guest at the charity fund-raising event?

'Come on,' Ryan called from the doorway. He frowned when he saw how pale Isobel had gone. 'Are you okay? You look like you've seen a ghost.' He glanced at her phone as she dropped it into her bag. 'You haven't had any more nuisance calls, have you?'

It wouldn't be fair to share her worries about the stalker with Ryan tonight, when he was clearly ecstatic that his girlfriend had agreed to marry him. There was probably nothing to worry about anyway. She was being silly to let the mysterious David bother her.

She shrugged. 'I told you, I've just got a bit of stage fright, that's all,' she said as they took the lift down to the ground floor of the hotel. 'In a strange way I find it more daunting to perform in front of an audience of five hundred guests who paid a fortune for tickets, than at an arena in front of thousands of fans.'

Keen to take her mind away from the unsettling phone call, she changed the subject. 'Are you and Emily going to announce your engagement tonight?'

'No, I only proposed yesterday, and she's gone to her parents' country estate in Suffolk to break the news to them first.' As they walked backstage to wait until it was time for the band's performance Ryan caught hold of Isobel's hand. 'Thanks for helping me and Emily to keep our relationship out of the media. The speculation that you and I are romantically involved has allowed Emily to stay out of the limelight.'

They were interrupted by one of the sound technicians. 'You're on in two minutes, guys and girls. Do you want to check your mic, Izzy?'

As the host for the evening walked onto the stage to introduce the Stone Ladies, Isobel peeped through a gap in the curtains and felt a sickening sensation in the pit of her stomach. The glare of the footlights meant that it was impossible for her to see the audience clearly, but even if she could make out people's faces she would not recognise David. He had told her in one of his phone calls that they had met after a Stone Ladies concert and she had given him her autograph, but since the band had become famous Isobel had met hundreds of fans and signed her autograph countless times. She assumed David must have asked her to write 'to my darling'—fans often made strange requests—but she had no recollection of him.

Was he out there in the audience? She shivered as she remembered his most recent phone call. What had he meant when he'd said that they were destined to be together for ever? Was it her overactive imagination, or had there been something vaguely threatening in his words?'

The curtains were opening and there were cheers from the audience, but Isobel's feet felt as though they were rooted to the spot. The urge to run from the stage was so strong that she half turned and bumped into Ryan, who was standing behind her.

'Forget everything else and just focus on the music,' he murmured. 'Pretend we're kids again, four friends pretending to be rock stars in Eckerton village hall.'

Ryan's words calmed her and she looked around at Carly and Ben and returned their smiles. During her marriage, she had tried to explain to Constantin that the band had become her family who gave her the love and affection that she hadn't received from her father. After she had lost her baby, it had been her closest friends who had supported her through the darkest days of her life because Constantin had refused to talk about what had happened.

Taking a deep breath, she walked out onto the stage and launched into a song that had recently been a number-one hit in the charts. There was applause from the audience, but Isobel blocked out everything else and sank into the music. Ever since she had been a small child and had picked out simple tunes on her mother's piano, music had been her great love, her joy and her solace when she had needed an outlet for her emotions.

'…Constantin?'

The sound of his name intruded on Constantin's thoughts, and he tore his eyes away from the unedifying spectacle of his wife dancing with her *very* good friend, Ryan Fellows. A nerve flickered in his jaw, but a lifetime of disguising his true emotions came to his rescue and he smiled smoothly at the willowy blonde at his side, who was staring at him accusingly.

'I'm sure you haven't been listening to me!'

Lying was pointless. The woman—Ginny? Jenny? he'd already forgotten her name—had sat next to him during dinner and seemed to think that she had exclusive rights to his attention for the rest of the evening. But ignoring her had been rude. He gave an apologetic shrug of his shoulders. 'Forgive me. I have things on my mind and I'm afraid I am not an attentive companion tonight. But I'm sure there are many other men here who would enjoy meeting you,' he murmured.

The blonde finally took the hint and flounced away. Constantin watched the indignant sway of her bottom clad in tight red satin for all of two seconds, before his eyes were drawn back to the dance floor and Isobel.

Listening to her singing earlier in the evening, he had been struck anew by the liquid quality of her voice, and he had been reminded of a crystal-clear stream tumbling softly over pebbles. He had never understood when she had said that music was part of her. But watching her on the stage tonight, he'd realised that she sang from her heart, from the depths of her soul, and he had felt an inexplicable ache in his chest, a longing for something that might have been, if he had been a different man.

His gaze narrowed on the man who was dancing with Isobel. Constantin presumed that women found the long-haired guitarist attractive. Certainly Fellows and Isobel made a striking couple. Were they already lovers or would she at least have the decency to wait until she was free of her marriage before taking another man to her bed? Violent rage simmered in his gut. The potency of his jealousy terrified him, but he could not control it.

Was this how his father had felt when he had watched his young second wife laughing with her friends? Had Franco De Severino been overcome by murderous rage when he and Lorena had argued on the balcony that fateful day?

Sweat beaded on Constantin's brow. He knew he should not have accepted the invitation to tonight's event once he'd learned that the Stone Ladies would be attending. His brain told him he should get out of there, *fast*, but his feet were already carrying him swiftly across the dance floor in Isobel's direction.

Was David somewhere in the ballroom watching her? Isobel could not dismiss the thought as her mind replayed the stalker's unnerving phone call. During the Stone Ladies' performance she had managed to forget about him, but her tension had returned when she'd left the stage and joined the party guests. She told herself she was overreacting. The stalker had not actually threatened to harm her. But she could not shake off her feeling of unease, and she had stayed close to Ryan all evening.

'Don't look,' he murmured in her ear as he guided her around the dance floor, 'but an extremely dangerous-looking man is heading our way.'

Isobel's heart lurched. 'What do you mean? What man?' Was David going to reveal himself? She gripped Ryan's arm.

'It's Constantin, and I get the distinct impression that he'd like to tear me limb from limb. I thought you said it was all over between the two of you.'

'It is…' The words died on Isobel's lips as she felt a heavy hand on her shoulder and she was spun round to find Constantin's darkly handsome face looming above her. The fear she'd felt when she had believed she was going to be confronted by the man who had been terrorising her with phone calls was replaced by a different kind of tension as Constantin stepped between her and Ryan.

'Excuse me, Fellows,' he drawled in a deceptively soft voice that resonated with menace. 'It's my turn to dance with my wife.'

Ryan looked uncertain. 'Is that okay with you, Izzy?'

It was on the tip of her tongue to say that she would rather walk over hot coals than dance with Constantin, but the determined gleam in her husband's eyes made her swallow her words. She did not want to cause a scene, especially as she knew that members of the press were at the party and would love to report a fracas on the dance floor. Anyway, she had no time to appeal to Ryan for help because Constantin clamped his hands on her waist and whisked her away.

'What the hell are you playing at?' she demanded, but

the asperity in her voice was muffled as he slid his arms around her and drew her towards him so that her face was pressed against his chest. Beneath his crisp white shirt she could see the shadow of his dark chest hairs, and the heat from his body and the spicy scent of his aftershave intoxicated her senses. It had to be at this moment that the upbeat disco music changed to a slow ballad, she thought despairingly.

She tilted her head so that she could look at him. 'Why are you here?'

'I accepted an invitation to support the fund-raising event for a worthwhile charity.' His eyes met hers, and the glitter in his cobalt gaze sent molten heat surging through Isobel's veins. 'I also knew that you would be here,' he admitted. 'Your visit last week made me re-evaluate our situation and I concluded that you were right when you pointed out that there were many good things about our relationship.

She stared at him in confusion. 'So, what are you saying?'

'I'm saying that I've changed my mind about the divorce. I think we should give our marriage another chance.'

Isobel's shock gave way to anger. 'Just like that, you've *changed your mind*? You've got a nerve, Constantin.' It was typical of Constantin not to give an explanation but to expect her to simply accept his decision, and no doubt welcome him back into her life with open arms. 'Last week you were adamant that we should divorce. What happened that brought about this miraculous change of heart?' she asked sarcastically.

As she'd climbed into a taxi and driven away from the house in Grosvenor Square a week ago, she had vowed that her tears were the last she would shed over Constantin, and a clean break was the only sensible thing to do.

Suddenly it was all too much: the romantic music, the way Constantin was holding her close to his body so that she could feel the steady beat of his heart beneath his ribcage and—she caught her breath as he pressed his hand into the small of her back—the hard ridge of his arousal jabbing into her thigh.

Her brain was sending out an urgent warning that she must step away from him, but desire was unfurling in the pit of her stomach and she was trapped by the sensual heat in his eyes as he bent his head towards her.

'This happened, Isabella,' he whispered against her lips. 'We are both prisoners of the incredible passion that exists between us—that has always existed since the moment we first set eyes on each other. When we met last week it was all we could do not to tear each other's clothes off. You weren't the only one to imagine making love on the gym mat,' he drawled in an amused voice as she opened her mouth to deny the erotic images that had crowded her mind when she had watched him working out.

'I don't want...' she began desperately, but the rest of her words were crushed beneath his mouth.

'Yes, *bella*, you do. And so do I,' Constantin told her firmly, and proceeded to demonstrate his mastery with a kiss that plumbed the depths of her soul as he took without mercy and demanded a response that Isobel was unable to deny him.

CHAPTER FOUR

IT HAD BEEN so long since Constantin had held her in his arms and kissed her with mind-blowing passion. The years of heartache fell away and Isobel trembled as he increased the pressure of his lips on hers, evoking a hunger inside her that had lain dormant until he had reawakened her desire with one look from his glittering blue eyes. A tiny part of her mind warned that she must resist the wanton warmth flooding through her body, but as Constantin pulled her even closer so that she could feel the hardness of his arousal press against her pelvis she gave up the fight with herself and succumbed to his sensual demands.

The voices of the party guests, the clink of glasses, faded, and there was only the music and the man who retained the key to her heart. She was barely aware of her feet touching the floor as Constantin swept her around the dance floor. His mouth did not leave hers, but the tenor of his kiss altered and became so sweetly beguiling that tears filled her eyes. She felt as if she had come home after a long journey, and as he deepened the kiss to something that was flagrantly sensual the ache of loneliness in her heart eased.

'Get a room!' Laughter followed the raucous comment, and Isobel was catapulted back to reality. She snatched her mouth from Constantin's and looked around wildly, horrified to find that they were the only couple on the dance floor, and they were being observed by an avid audience. The flash of a camera bulb brought home to her just what a fool she had been.

'The press are going to love this,' she muttered. She shot Constantin a sharp glance and felt infuriated by his amused expression. 'Pictures of us will be in the newspapers tomorrow. It won't take journalists long to discover that we are married, and they'll be curious to know why we've lived apart for the last two years.'

He shrugged. 'Why is that a problem? We'll simply explain that our relationship went through a difficult patch, but now we are back together.'

'But we're not!' Her eyes narrowed suspiciously. 'You set me up, didn't you? You deliberately made a…a public spectacle of us because for some reason you've suddenly decided that we should be reconciled.' She touched her mouth with shaking fingers and cringed when she felt its swollen contours. Why on earth had she allowed Constantin to kiss her, to *ravish* her, in such a public display?

Isobel's words came uncomfortably close to the truth for Constantin. His jaw hardened. 'I didn't hear you object when I kissed you, *cara*.'

Sickening shame swept through her at his soft taunt. Without another word she spun round and marched off the dance floor, but her high heels and long dress hampered her progress and Constantin's long stride easily kept pace with her as she walked out of the ballroom.

'Go away,' she demanded in a fierce undertone as she crossed the lobby. She was desperate to escape the curious glances of the other guests, and as she hurried down the hotel steps she prayed for a taxi to appear.

'My car is over there.' Constantin nodded towards the

sports car parked a little way down the street. 'I'll drive you home.'

'I'd rather wait for a taxi.' She was furious with him, but even more so with herself for allowing him to think she was a pushover. The bitter truth was that she did not dare risk being alone with him, she acknowledged.

The glare of a flashbulb momentarily blinded her, and her heart sank as a reporter whom she recognised from one of the tabloids thrust a microphone at her. 'Izzy, what's the story about you and Constantin De Severino?' The reporter looked curiously at Constantin. 'Have you split with Ryan Fellows, and, if so, what does it mean for the future of the Stone Ladies?'

How was it that a taxi never appeared when you wanted one? she thought, frustrated.

'Do you want to stand here and talk to this jerk, or do you want to go home?' Constantin spoke in her ear.

The arrival of two more reporters decided the matter for her and she quickly followed him over to his car and slid into the passenger seat. Seconds later, the powerful engine roared into life and Constantin accelerated away from the kerb.

'Is your address still the apartment block near Tower Bridge?' When she had left him, Constantin had offered to buy her a place of her own to live, but stubborn Isobel had refused his help and had proudly told him that she was able to pay for a flat with money she had earned from the Stone Ladies' first hit record. She had often accused him of being remote and cold during their marriage, but whenever he *had* tried to build bridges, her prickly independence had come to the fore and she had seemed reluctant to accept anything from him.

Isobel gave a nod of confirmation. She looked over her shoulder as a camera flashbulb shone through the car's rear window. 'See what you've done?' she rounded on him angrily. 'Our so-called relationship is going to feature in all the gossip columns. I'll have to warn Ryan,' she muttered. 'It might make things awkward.'

Constantin frowned. 'You mean it will be awkward when the press report that you are married to me at the same time as you've been carrying on with Fellows? My heart bleeds for you, *cara*,' he said sarcastically.

'I haven't been *carrying on* with Ryan. I've told you a hundred times that he and I are just friends.'

'You have never denied in interviews that the two of you are having an affair.' Constantin's hands tightened on the steering wheel as he recalled how Isobel had been glued to the guitarist's side at the party. 'It's obvious that you have a close relationship with him.'

Isobel's temper boiled over and she threw her hands up in the air in a gesture of angry frustration. '*Yes*, I admit I'm close to him. I love Ryan—but as a brother, not a lover. And he…he has tried to fill the place of the brother I lost.' She could not control the tremor in her voice.

Constantin shot her a puzzled look. 'I didn't know you had a brother. You've never spoken of him before. Your parents made no mention that they had a son when we visited them in Derbyshire.'

Isobel bit her lip as she remembered the one and only occasion that Constantin had met her parents. They hadn't attended the wedding because her father had been too unwell to travel to London. After she and Constantin had returned from their honeymoon, they had driven through the picturesque Peak District, before arriving at the far less attractive village of Eckerton, where rows of ugly terraced miners' cottages stood in the shadow of the abandoned colliery.

Her mother had been overawed by Constantin and kept

up a stream of nervous chatter as she had served tea from her best china. Her father had been his usual, dour self and had barely uttered a word. Looking around the tiny sitting room, with its threadbare carpet and old furniture, Isobel had shuddered to imagine what Constantin had made of her childhood home and her unwelcoming father. The visit had emphasised the huge social divide between her and the enigmatic Italian aristocrat she had married.

'They never speak of Simon. He died in an accident when he was fourteen and my father wouldn't allow my mother or me to mention his name, or even have photos of him on the wall. I suppose it was Dad's way of dealing with the tragedy of losing his son. You dealt with the loss of our baby in the same way, by refusing to talk about Arianna.' Her voice was husky with emotions that she was struggling to suppress.

A nerve flickered in Constantin's jaw, but he ignored her jibe. 'What happened to your brother?'

'It was a scorching hot summer's day and Simon and a group of his friends decided to swim in the reservoir near to where we lived. Actually, it was Ryan who suggested it and he has never forgiven himself. My brother was a daredevil, and while some of the boys went into the water and stayed close to the bank, Simon swam out of his depth. It's thought that he had an attack of cramp. Ryan said that he was fine one minute but then he suddenly started shouting for help. By the time Ryan had swum out to him, Simon had disappeared below the surface. Somehow Ryan managed to grab hold of him and drag him back to the shore. He tried to resuscitate him, but he was unable to save him…and Simon died.'

It was difficult to talk past the lump in her throat. 'Afterwards, Ryan became severely depressed. He felt guilty that Simon had swum in the reservoir. But what happened wasn't Ryan's fault. Simon always pushed the boundaries, and it was typical of him to have swum out of his depth. I didn't blame Ryan. He and my brother were best friends and Simon's death forged a bond between us that will always remain. But friendship is *all* there is between me and Ryan. He is in love with his girlfriend and he and Emily are planning to get married.'

'If that's true, why didn't the pair of you scotch the rumours of an affair?'

She shrugged. 'We told the truth when we said that we are good friends. The press decided that there must be more to our relationship, and we didn't deny the rumours because, while attention was on us, it allowed Ryan's girlfriend to escape the media's interest.' Isobel hesitated. 'I guess it is okay to tell you, as Ryan is going to make a public announcement in the next day or so. Emily's father is a well-known politician and a member of the government. If it had become known that Ryan was dating her, they would have been constantly followed by the paparazzi.'

'So, being a loyal friend, you allowed the speculation about your relationship with Fellows to continue,' Constantin said grimly. 'You did not care if I heard the rumours that my wife was involved with another man. Didn't you think you owed *me,* your husband, your loyalty?'

'Not when hardly a week went by without a picture of you with a different beautiful woman in the newspapers. How dare you accuse me of disloyalty when you paraded the members of your…your *harem* in public?'

Isobel jerked her eyes from him and stared out of the car window, breathing hard. She was not going to admit how hurt she had felt when she'd seen pictures of Constantin with other women. If she was scrupulously honest with herself, she had not denied to the press the rumours of an affair with Ryan because she had hoped that Constantin would realise that she wasn't pining for him.

The simmering tension inside the car stretched her nerves to snapping point, and she felt relieved when he parked outside her apartment building.

'Thanks for the lift.' She glanced at his handsome profile and bit her lip. 'I don't understand why you said you've changed your mind about the divorce. Separating permanently is the only sensible thing to do. Our marriage is well and truly over. The truth is that it would have been better if we had never met,' she said in a low tone.

His head shot round and his blue eyes glittered fiercely. 'You don't mean that.'

If they had never met, she would never have held her tiny baby girl in her arms. Arianna had never lived in the world, but she lived on in Isobel's heart.

'We were good together.' Constantin's husky accent caused her stomach muscles to contract.

'In bed!' She gave a hollow laugh. 'But marriage has to have more than sex for it to work. Trust, for instance. You resented my friendships with the other members of the band. That's clear from the way you were so ready to believe I was having an affair with Ryan. Sometimes I had the feeling that you wished you could lock me away in a tower, away from all other human contact.' Her voice shook. 'And yet you were so remote and cold towards me that you can hardly blame me for wanting to be with my friends.'

An image flashed into Constantin's mind of his father and stepmother, and inside his head he heard Lorena's impassioned cry.

I feel smothered, Franco. You're jealous of my friends, and of any man I happen to glance at. You are even jealous of your own son!

Dio! Had Isobel felt smothered by *him,* just as Lorena had by his father? He had tried to fight his possessive feelings and the dark jealousy that he feared he had inherited from his father, but in doing so he had come across as cold and uncaring.

Isobel got out of the car and Constantin watched her walk towards the front door of the apartment building. She was exquisitely desirable in her gold dress that clung to her slender figure. 'Our marriage is well and truly over,' she had insisted. He frowned as he thought of his uncle's threat to appoint his cousin Maurio as Chairman of DSE.

Nothing was going to stop him from claiming the position that was rightfully his.

Growling a curse, he flung open the car door and strode after his wife.

He caught up with her as she stood on the top step and searched in her bag for her door key. 'Invite me in, Isabella, so that we can talk.'

'We have nothing to talk about.' Isobel located her key in the bottom of her bag and gripped it tightly. Her composure was near to breaking point, and she was desperate to reach her flat before she did something stupid like fling her arms around Constantin and beg him to hold her close and never let her go. Her eyes were drawn to his, and the sensual heat in his gaze made her tremble. 'We're no good for each other,' she whispered.

'Not true, *tesorino.*'

His use of the affectionate term that he had often spoken to her at the beginning of their marriage undermined her defences, and she was unprepared when he slid his arm around her waist and pulled her towards him.

His dark head descended and he claimed her lips, kissing her with a fiery passion that lit a flame inside Isobel. *This* had always been good for both of them, she acknowledged. Sex—white-hot and wickedly erotic! She had been inexperienced when she had met Constantin but he had discovered her secret desires and had used his knowledge mercilessly to take her repeatedly to a sensual nirvana.

She was melting inside. Heat flooded between her thighs and her body was impatient for more, *more* of the exquisite pleasure promised by the bold sweep of Constantin's tongue inside her mouth. She wanted him. She would always want him, she thought despairingly. But he was no good for her.

He traced his lips over her cheek and the slender arch of her neck. 'Invite me in,' he murmured in her ear. 'Let me remind you of how good we are together.'

'No!' Determination not to take a path that she knew would lead to heartache gave her the strength to push him away. 'Sex isn't the solution. In our case, it was the problem,' she said shakily. 'We were drawn together by desire, and if we had just had an affair it would probably have burned out as quickly as your affairs with other women. When I fell pregnant you felt obliged to marry me.' She smiled sadly. 'I'll never forget Arianna, but it's time we both moved on with our lives, Constantin.'

That was easy for Isobel to say, he thought grimly. The Stone Ladies were hugely successful, but his career at DSE, his *life* for heaven's sake, was about to go into free-fall unless he could persuade her to come back to him. He didn't doubt that he *could* persuade her back into his bed. He had felt her tremble when he'd kissed her and knew she shared his hunger. If he drew her back into his arms, he was confident that she would offer little resistance. But his conscience stayed him. Her clear hazel eyes reflected her confusion. Undoubtedly she desired him. But for her, it wasn't enough, and Constantin knew he was no more capable of satisfying her emotional needs now than he had been two years ago.

As Isobel shut the front door on Constantin and walked across the lobby to the lift, she assured herself that she was relieved he had not tried to detain her. She knew she had been right to turn down having sex with him, but her body did not agree and the dragging ache in the pit of her stomach was almost as bad as the ache in her heart.

'Evening, Miss Blake,' the concierge greeted her. 'The parcel that you said you were expecting to be delivered didn't arrive today.'

'I'll have to phone the courier tomorrow. Goodnight, Albert.'

As the lift carried her to the fourth floor she focused her thoughts on the missing parcel, the friend she'd arranged to meet for lunch the following day, anything but Constantin. Her life was good the way it was. Why alter the status quo and allow him to turn her world upside down again?

She had no idea why he had suddenly decided that he didn't want a divorce. There was a time when she would have immediately given in to him, in the desperate hope that perhaps he did have feelings for her. She had been pathetic, Isobel thought grimly. But after she'd had the miscarriage Constantin had let her down badly by failing to support her. She was no longer in awe of him, and, although she had a sneaking suspicion that she would always be in love with him, she understood that he was an ordinary mortal—a complex man, certainly, but he had his faults just as she did. Unfortunately she simply could not believe that they would be able to resolve the differences that had driven them apart.

The lift stopped and the doors opened. The front door of her flat was a couple of hundred yards along the corridor. Isobel glanced down to select the appropriate key on the key ring she was holding, when something, a sixth sense, warned her that she wasn't alone.

'Who's there…?' She looked over her shoulder down the brightly lit, empty corridor, and cursed her overactive imagination.

'Hello, Izzy.'

She spun round, and her heart cannoned into her ribs as a man stepped out from a shadowed recess and walked towards her. She did not know him, but she had recognised his voice. 'David?'

He was shortish, thinnish—nondescript. For a moment Isobel wondered why she had been so worried about this very ordinary-looking, middle-aged man.

'I knew you must remember me.' He smiled pleasantly. 'You felt the connection between us when we met at a Stone Ladies concert. We were together in a previous world and we will be together again in the next one, my darling.'

The strange expression in his eyes sent a frisson of fear through Isobel, and she sensed that beneath his outwardly benign manner he was a mass of nervous energy and excitement that she found unnerving.

'I bought these for you.' It was only then that she registered he was holding a cardboard box. Something in the man's demeanour told Isobel to remain calm and play along with him. Hoping he did not notice that her hands were shaking, she took the box from him and opened the lid. The sickly-sweet scent of oriental lilies that pervaded the air was so strong she almost gagged.

Feeling that he expected a response from her, she murmured, 'They're lovely.' She stared at the white flowers and repressed a shudder.

'You remind me of a lily, beautiful and pure.' David's voice suddenly changed. 'I thought you were pure, until I watched you kissing another man tonight.'

Isobel swallowed. 'You were there…at the party?'

'Where else would I be but with you, my angel? You belong to *me*, Izzy, and no other man shall try to steal you from me.'

Isobel tensed as the stalker took a step closer. Her key was digging into the palm of her hand and she glanced along the corridor, trying to estimate the distance to her front door, wondering what her chances were of getting past David and making it to the safety of her flat. She did not dare risk it. Although he was not physically imposing, she sensed that he was stronger than he looked. His pale eyes were watching her intently and the manic gleam in his gaze chilled her blood.

'Come away with me.' His voice hardened when she shook her head. 'It is time that you and I left this earthly world.'

The hell it was! Isobel's survival instinct kicked in. She threw the box of lilies at the stalker's face before she spun round and raced down the corridor. Of course the flowers were not a substantial weapon, but her actions had surprised him and given her a vital few seconds' head start. She heard his angry shout, heard his footsteps as he chased after her, but she resisted the temptation to look behind her as she reached the lift, which was thankfully still waiting at the fourth floor. She hit the button to open the doors. Come on, *come on!* she pleaded as they slid apart agonisingly slowly. She heard heavy breathing close to her, and she screamed as a hand grabbed her bare shoulder.

In desperation she rammed her elbow hard into the stalker's stomach. He groaned and released his grip. She fell into the lift and held down the button to close the doors. Only then did she look round and glimpse his crazed expression before the metal doors obliterated him from view.

As the lift descended she tried to marshal her thoughts.

How had David gained entry to the apartment building? The concierge always vetted visitors, and some of her friends had joked that it would be easier to break into the Bank of England than slip past Albert. Reaction was setting in, and she felt sick as the lift arrived at ground level.

'Miss Blake?' The concierge looked up from his desk. 'Is something the matter?'

Isobel did not reply. Through the glass doors of the building she saw Constantin's tall figure illuminated by the street lamp. He was not looking in her direction as he lowered his mobile phone from his ear and walked towards his car. Impelled by an instinct she did not even try to question, she flew across the lobby.

'Constantin—*wait*!'

The sound of Isobel's voice drew Constantin's thoughts from the phone conversation he'd just had with the finance director at the New York office. The East Coast of the USA was five hours behind England, and Jeff Zuckerman had seemed blithely unconcerned that it was midnight in London.

Constantin glanced round and dismissed work issues from his mind when he saw Isobel running towards him. Her blonde hair spilled over her shoulders and he felt a tightening in his groin as he watched the bounce of her firm breasts as she ran.

'Have you changed your mind about inviting me up to your flat, Isabella?' His smile disappeared along with his sense of pleasurable anticipation when he saw the look of terror on her face. '*Santa Madre!*' He caught her as she literally threw herself into his arms and held her tightly as tremors shook her body. 'What the hell...?'

'He was waiting for me outside my flat. He's so weird.' Her words were jumbled and incoherent. 'He wanted me to go with him, and he gave me funeral flowers.'

Constantin cupped her chin and tilted her face to his. '*Who* was waiting for you, *cara*?'

'David…the man who has been stalking me.' Isobel released her breath on a ragged sigh as the fear drained out of her. She felt safe with Constantin. It did not even occur to her that her blind trust in him revealed perhaps too much of her deepest feelings.

'*Stalking you?*' Constantin's eyes glittered fiercely. 'Do you mean to say that your safety has been threatened by this man? For how long has this been going on? Why didn't you tell me? I would have arranged security measures, hired a bodyguard to protect you.'

'I don't need a bodyguard.' The stark terror that had gripped Isobel when David had confronted her outside her flat seemed like an overreaction now, and she felt embarrassed that she had involved Constantin. The determined set of his jaw warned her that he would not let up until she had told him everything.

'I've been getting nuisance calls from a man called David for a few months. I've changed my landline number and mobile-phone number, but somehow he managed to get hold of my new numbers.

'He said we had met at a Stone Ladies concert…but I don't remember meeting him. He phoned me just before I went on stage tonight and said that he would be watching me tonight.' She bit her lip. 'I spent all evening wondering if one of the guests was the stalker. When I stepped out of the lift after you'd brought me home he appeared in the corridor.'

The memory of David's wild-eyed expression sent a shiver through Isobel. 'He said it was time that he and I left this earthly world. I'm not sure what he meant.' She hadn't waited around to find out, she thought, and shivered again.

A nerve flickering in Constantin's jaw was the only

indication of his barely restrained fury. Give him two minutes alone with the guy who got his kicks out of frightening Isobel, and the stalker wouldn't be able to walk, let alone *stalk* a defenceless woman, he thought grimly. The glimmer of tears in Isobel's eyes and the realisation that she was not nearly as calm as she was pretending to be stopped him from rushing up to the fourth floor to look for the intruder.

He pulled his phone from his pocket. 'I'll call the police.'

'I'll do it,' Isobel said shakily. 'I have a direct number to report any incidents with the stalker.'

The terror she had felt when David had accosted her was fading, and she felt angry with herself for not telling the man to get lost. He was probably a harmless overenthusiastic fan, she told herself, although the wild expression in his eyes suggested the possibility that he had mental-health issues.

She remained in the lobby with Albert while Constantin went up to the fourth floor. The concierge was adamant that no one fitting the stalker's description had entered the apartment building, and he was deeply upset when he explained that the CCTV system had developed a fault and was due to be repaired the next day.

The police arrived to take a statement. An officer joined Constantin in searching every floor of the apartment block, but all they found were a few white lily petals. 'The intruder must have somehow accessed the building by the fire escape,' the police officer in charge told Isobel. 'It's a pity for us and lucky for him that the CCTV is down or we would have his face on film.'

Because the stalker had not assaulted her, or made a specific threat to harm her, there was little more that the police could do except to advise Isobel on measures she

should take to ensure her personal safety. While she was
giving her statement she saw Constantin walk out of the
flat. She assumed he felt he had done all that he could to
help her, but she wished he had stayed a few minutes longer so that she could have thanked him.

After the police had gone, she purposefully concen-
trated on the mundane tasks of removing her make-up
and washing her face, before exchanging the gold evening
gown for her favourite item of nightwear—namely one of
Constantin's tee shirts that she had taken with her when
she had called time on their marriage. Despite her best
efforts not to think about the stalker, the memory of his
strangeness lingered in her mind, and although she knew
she was being ridiculous she checked inside the wardrobe
and the hall cupboard to make sure he had not somehow
gained entry to her flat.

There was no question of trying to sleep. She would
make a milky drink and watch TV for a while. Walking
into the sitting room, she stopped dead and drew a sharp
breath.

'How did you get in here?'

CHAPTER FIVE

CONSTANTIN HAD DISCARDED his tuxedo and tie and unfastened the top buttons on his shirt to reveal the bronzed skin of his throat, and a few curling black chest hairs. He was leaning back against the sofa cushions, his long legs stretched out in front of him and his arms crossed behind his head in an attitude of indolent relaxation that was far removed from the stomach-squirming tension that gripped Isobel as she stared at his handsome face.

'I saw you leave and assumed you had gone home.'

'I went to get something from my car and borrowed your door key so that I could let myself back into the flat. You were talking to the police officer, and I guess you didn't notice me go into the kitchen.' He nodded to the cup and saucer on the coffee table. 'I made you a cup of tea.'

Isobel was less interested in the tea than the holdall on the floor by his feet.

'I always keep an overnight bag in the car,' he explained, following her gaze, 'in case I decide to stay away from home for some reason.'

No doubt 'some reason' meant an invitation from a woman to spend the night together. Isobel felt a shaft of pain at the idea of him making love to one of the numerous gorgeous females he had been photographed with in the newspapers during the past two years. Jealousy burned hotly inside her—another unwanted emotion to add to the list of unpleasant experiences tonight, she thought grimly.

The discernible gleam of amusement in his eyes was the last straw. She gave him a tight smile. 'I hope you find somewhere comfortable to stay tonight.'

He laughed softly and patted the cushion. 'I'm sure your sofa is very comfortable. I'll let you know in the morning.'

'There's absolutely no reason for you to stay.' Constantin made her feel more unnerved than David did, albeit in a different way, Isobel thought ruefully. 'I'll put the double lock on the front door, and, unless the stalker is Spiderman, he won't be able to climb through a window on the fourth floor.'

Constantin merely gave her a lazy smile. 'Humour me, hmm, *cara*?'

'This is ridiculous. I don't want you here.' Her tone was unknowingly desperate. He unsettled her way too much for *her* comfort.

He stood up and strolled towards her. Isobel sensed that beneath his laid-back manner he was utterly determined to have his own way. 'If I leave, I will demand the immediate return of my personal property, which you took without my consent.'

'What personal property…?' She stiffened as he took hold of the hem of her tee shirt, *his* tee shirt. The shirt reached to just below her hips, and the light brush of his fingers against her thigh felt as if a flame had burned her flesh. Her breath caught in her throat as he slowly began to raise the hem.

'You really want this old shirt back?' she said in a choked voice.

'I particularly like this shirt.'

If he continued to lift the tee shirt up he would reveal her bare breasts. She gave a little shiver—half excitement and half apprehension—as she imagined him stripping her and cupping her breasts in his hands. She would be a fool to take this route again, but when had she ever behaved sensibly where Constantin was concerned?

Constantin was tempted to whip the shirt over her head and then pull her close, trace his hands over her body to rediscover every delicious dip and curve before taking the same path with his mouth. It was how they had always communicated best, two bodies joined and moving in perfect accord. The suspicious brightness in Isobel's eyes warned him that her emotions were on a knife-edge. The stalker had scared her more than she had admitted to him or the police, and what she needed from him now was not passion but compassion.

'Stop fighting me, Isabella,' he said gently. 'You know you won't win. Sit down and drink your tea before it gets cold.'

If she didn't feel like a wrung-out rag she would tell him where to go, Isobel thought. But she must be suffering from delayed shock or something because her legs refused to support her and she sat down abruptly. She wished she had chosen an armchair when Constantin joined her on the sofa, and she sipped her tea, trying to ignore her awareness of him.

'I was looking at your photos,' he remarked, glancing at the montage of photographs on the wall.

'I've kept a pictorial record of every city where the Stone Ladies have performed.' She recognised his ploy to keep her mind off the stalker and went along with it. 'Often we only play at a venue for one night before moving on to the next town but I have a list of places I'd like to go back and visit properly.'

'I've always wondered about the name of the band,' he

mused. 'Why did you call yourselves Stone Ladies when two of the band members are male?'

She smiled, and Constantin was glad to see evidence that some of her tension had eased. 'The name refers to an ancient stone circle on the moors near to the village in Derbyshire where we all grew up. The legend says that a group of ladies from the royal court loved to dance so much that they risked the wrath of the king by dancing on the Sabbath, and as a penalty they were turned to stone.

'Our group, Carly, Ben, Ryan and I, felt a lot of sympathy for the ladies because we had similar difficulties playing our music when we wanted to. None of us were allowed to practise at home.' She sighed. 'My father thought I should be studying, not singing, and Ryan's father expected him to spend all his spare time working on the family farm. Our parents couldn't understand how much our music meant to us. I had countless arguments with my father, who thought music was a waste of time and that I should focus on passing my exams and getting a proper job.'

The bleakness in her voice caught Constantin's attention. 'Your father must be proud of you now that you and the band are so successful?'

'Dad died a few months ago.' Isobel shrugged. 'He wasn't interested in my music or how well the band was doing. I couldn't live up to the expectations he'd had of me.'

'What do you mean?'

'My brother was Dad's favourite. Simon was really clever at school and had planned to go to university and train to be a doctor. My father was so proud of his son and he was devastated when Simon died. I'm afraid I was no substitute. I wasn't interested in academic subjects and Dad ridiculed my dreams of making a living as a musician. I couldn't be the person my father wanted me to be.'

She glanced at Constantin. 'When we married, I couldn't be the person *you* wanted me to be, either,' she said flatly.

He frowned. 'I did not have expectations of you. When we married I thought, *hoped* that you would be happy to fulfil the role of my wife.' His face darkened. 'But it wasn't enough for you.'

'What you wanted was a glamorous hostess who would organise dinner parties and impress your guests with her witty conversation and sublime sense of style,' Isobel said bitterly. 'I failed miserably as a hostess, and the designer clothes I wore were not *my* style, they were what you decided I should wear.'

'I admit there were occasions when your hippy-chick clothes were not suitable. DSE is synonymous with style and superb quality, and I needed my wife to help me to represent those qualities. The tie-dyed, flowers-in-your-hair look was not a good advertisement for the company,' he said sardonically.

'But it was *me*. The hippy look, as you call it, was *my* style. You didn't object to the way I dressed when we first met.'

He had not taken much notice of her clothes because he had been more interested in getting her out of them as quickly as possible, Constantin acknowledged cynically.

'You were determined to mould me into the perfect wife, in the same way that my father had tried to mould me into the perfect daughter,' Isobel rounded on him, her eyes flashing. 'But neither you nor my dad were interested in me as a person. And like my dad, you never showed any interest in my music or encouraged my singing career.'

His mouth tightened. 'When we were first married, you were not hell-bent on pursuing a music career. You've said yourself that we were happy living in London at the time, and you gave the impression that you were content to be a wife and soon-to-be mother to our child.'

His words sliced through Isobel's heart. 'But I didn't get the chance to be a mother.' Her voice was raw. 'It's true that in the early months of our marriage I was absorbed in my pregnancy,' and in *you*, she thought to herself, remembering the man she had married. Constantin had been a charming and attentive husband and she had let herself believe that her happiness would last.

'After we lost Arianna I was left with nothing. For reasons I didn't understand, you had become a remote stranger and I felt that I hardly knew you. All I had was my music. Writing songs and singing with the band were my only comfort in those terrible days when I sometimes wondered if I would go mad with grief.'

She swallowed the lump in her throat. Revisiting the past was always painful, but tonight, when her emotions were ragged after her scare with the stalker, being bombarded with memories was unendurable.

'This conversation is pointless,' she told Constantin as she jerked to her feet. 'We should have had it two years ago, but we didn't and now it's too late. One of the reasons I left was because you refused to talk about the things that mattered, like the miscarriage. You might have been able to forget about our baby but I felt desolate and unsupported by you.'

He leapt up and raked a hand through his hair. 'Perhaps we might have talked more if you had spent more time at home. I lost count of the number of times that I arrived home from work to be told by Whittaker that you were out with your friends.' His blue eyes glittered as cold and hard as sapphires. 'Don't put all the blame on me, Isobel. We couldn't work on the problems with our marriage because you were never there.'

She shook her head. 'It was you who was absent from our relationship. I don't mean in a physical sense, but on an emotional level you had distanced yourself from me. My friends gave me what you seemed incapable of giving—emotional support. You never allowed us the opportunity to *share* our feelings about the loss of our daughter. Even now, whenever I mention Arianna you clam up.'

'What's the point in going over and over it?' Constantin saw Isobel flinch at his raised voice and knew she was startled by his violent outburst, as well she might be, he thought grimly. He *never* lost control.

Only once in his life had he seen his father show emotion—on the day of Constantin's mother's funeral. He had been eight years old, and had managed to get through the church service and watching his mother's coffin being lowered into her grave without crying because he knew it was what was expected of him. 'De Severino men never cry,' his father had told him many times. But later, on his way up to bed, Constantin had heard a noise from his father's study, a sound like a wounded animal in great pain that had chilled his blood.

Peeping round the door, he had been startled to see his father lying curled up on the floor, sobbing uncontrollably. Franco's outpouring of grief had been shocking and terrifying to witness for an impressionable young boy. Constantin had felt sad that his mother had died, but his father's agony had scared him. At the age of eight he had decided that he never wanted to feel such pain. He never wanted to love so intensely that love's dark side, loss, would bring him to his knees.

He dragged his mind from the past and found Isobel staring at him with a bitter expression in her eyes.

She might have guessed that Constantin would not show

even a flicker of response to their daughter's name, Isobel thought angrily.

'You really are made of stone, aren't you? On the surface you are a man who has everything: looks, wealth, power, but you're an empty shell, Constantin. Inside, you are an emotional void and I actually feel sorry for you.'

Her words rankled. What did she know about the emotions he kept buried deep inside him? What did she really know about *him*? But the fact that she did not know him was his fault, taunted a voice inside Constantin's head. He had not dared open up the Pandora's box of his emotions to Isobel for fear of what he might reveal about himself.

He looked at her wearing the baggy tee shirt that disguised her shape, and was infuriated by the realisation that even if she wore a sack that covered her from head to toe he would still want her more than he had ever wanted any other woman. Goaded by the accusation in her eyes, and by the knowledge that he *had* failed her when she'd had the miscarriage, he shot out his hand and caught hold of her wrist.

'I don't need your pity, *mia bella*. There's only one thing I ever needed from you,' he told her, pulling her towards him. 'You keep saying that you wished we had talked more, but the truth is neither of us wanted to waste time talking because we were so damned hungry for each other.'

'Sex would not have solved our problems,' Isobel cried, panic filling her as she tried vainly to break free from him. In truth, his grip on her wrist was not very tight. It was his grip on her heart that prevented her escape.

As she watched his dark head descend she wondered if, when their marriage had been falling apart, sex might have been a solution that would have given them a way to communicate again. But ever since Constantin had suggested that they make love two months after the miscarriage, and she had rejected him, a chasm had opened up between them and he had not approached her again.

At the time she had been angry with him for what she had perceived as his lack of support. But perhaps he had been trying to reach out to her, she thought with hindsight. In bed they had always understood each other perfectly and their desire had been mutually explosive and fulfilling.

While her mind had once again been focused on the past, she had forgotten the danger of her present situation. When had Constantin unclamped his fingers from her wrist and slid his arm around her waist? Her breath rushed from her lungs as he tugged her against him, making her agonisingly aware of every hard muscle and sinew on his whipcord body as he locked his other arm around her. Her eyes flew to his face, but her demand for him to release her died in her throat as his mouth came down on hers and he made demands of his own, his kiss hot and potent and utterly ruthless in its mastery.

He moved one hand down to clasp her bottom, jerking her pelvis into burning contact with the solid ridge of his arousal. She found his dominance shamefully thrilling. Beneath his civilised façade Constantin was all primitive, passionate male. It had been so long since she had felt him inside her. The thought weakened her resolve to resist him and when he slipped his hand beneath the hem of her shirt and stroked his fingers over her stomach and ribcage, she held her breath and silently willed him to move his hand higher and touch her breasts.

He had always had the ability to read her mind, and when he brushed his thumb pad across one swollen nipple she gave a choked cry. He took advantage of her parted lips to push his tongue into her mouth. Isobel's senses were swamped by him. The scent of his cologne was achingly familiar. She remembered the first time he had made love to her; she had been overwhelmed by the responses he had drawn from her untutored body, and afterwards she had pressed her face into his neck and tasted salt on his sweat-sheened skin.

He transferred his hand to her other breast and rolled her nipple between his fingers, causing a shaft of exquisite sensation to shoot through her. With a soft moan she melted against him and tipped her head back as he traced his lips down her throat. Constantin pushed the neck of the too-big tee shirt over her shoulder and trailed kisses along her collarbone.

'Mio Dio!' His savage imprecation shattered the sensual mist as he stared at the livid red mark he had uncovered. 'What happened to your shoulder?'

Isobel had noticed the beginnings of the bruise while she had been undressing for bed, but when Constantin had kissed her she had forgotten everything but her need for him. 'He...the stalker caught hold of me as I ran for the lift, but I managed to get away from him.' She shivered as her mind flashed back to those terrifying moments before the lift doors had closed, when she had turned and seen David's face contorted with fury. She had tried to convince herself that he had meant her no harm, but the memory of his wild-eyed expression was stuck in her mind.

Constantin glimpsed the fear in Isobel's hazel eyes and felt a surge of anger at the stalker, but also at himself. *She had run to him for safety.* He choked back a mirthless laugh. The bitter truth was that, far from being safe with him, she was innocently unaware of the danger he posed to her. His—as it turned out—unfounded jealousy of Ryan Fellows was proof that he had inherited a dark side to his nature from his father. The monster that had been inside Franco De Severino also lived within Constantin and the only way to control the beast was to avoid awakening it.

So what the hell was he doing coming on to Isobel?

He stepped away from her and raked an unsteady hand through his hair. 'I'm going to stay here tonight,' he said roughly. She could argue all she liked, but the welt on her shoulder was a stark reminder of the terror she must have felt when the stalker had confronted her outside her flat.

He frowned as he remembered something she had said after the attack. 'What did you mean when you said that the stalker gave you funeral flowers?'

'Oh, the white lilies.' Isobel wondered if she had overreacted when the stalker had presented her with the flowers, and she felt silly that she'd mentioned them to Constantin. 'I don't suppose David meant anything sinister, but I've always hated lilies since my brother's funeral. The church was filled with them. My strongest memory of that awful day was the sickly perfume of lilies.' She shuddered. 'Since then I've always considered it the scent of death.'

'I had no idea you disliked them,' Constantin said slowly. He remembered that he had taken a bouquet of lilies to Isobel in the hospital after she'd had the miscarriage. Of course, giving her flowers had been a totally inadequate gesture when she had lost their baby, but he hadn't known what else to do. He had felt helpless to comfort her in her grief. Standing outside her room listening to her sobbing had ripped his heart to shreds. But from boyhood he had learned from his father to suppress his emotions. He had been unable to respond to Isobel the way she had needed him to, and was incapable of voicing his own devastation at the loss of their baby girl.

When he had found the bouquet of lilies had been stuffed into the rubbish bin he had taken it as a sign that Isobel blamed him for the miscarriage. The trip to Italy had been his idea, but it had been disastrous for so many reasons, he remembered grimly. She had rejected the flowers and it had felt as though she were rejecting him. But now it occurred to him that perhaps she had thrown the lilies away because she'd been unable to cope with the sad memories they evoked of her brother.

He glanced at her pale face and then at his watch, shocked to see that it was two a.m. 'You'd better try and get some sleep. You're safe, and no one can hurt you tonight.'

Isobel stifled a bitter laugh. Was Constantin unaware that his abrupt rejection a few moments ago was a hundred times more painful than the injury the stalker had inflicted on her? His chiselled features revealed no emotion. Clearly he had been unaffected when he had kissed her and maybe had even been amused by her eager response to him.

She flushed, remembering how her body had betrayed her, and an idea crept into her mind that perhaps he had deliberately set out to humiliate her. Suddenly it was all too much. *He* was too much. She did not want him here in her flat, but she knew him well enough to realise that she would be wasting her breath if she asked him to leave. 'You'll find a spare pillow and blanket in the hall cupboard,' she told him, proud that her steady voice did not reveal her inner turmoil.

Without sparing him another glance, she walked down the hall to her bedroom and shut the door, wishing that she could lock it. But the likelihood that Constantin would enter her bedroom was zero, she reminded herself, thinking of how he had pulled back from making love to her. Reaction to the night's events was setting in and she felt bone weary. Her last thought as she lay back on the pillows was that it was too late to recapture the fleeting happiness they had once shared.

* * *

Isobel's sofa was probably very comfortable as a sofa, but as a makeshift bed for a man of six feet four it failed to provide a good night's sleep. But perhaps his restless night could not be entirely blamed on the sofa, Constantin acknowledged fairly as he stood up and ran a hand over the dark stubble covering his jaw. The insistent throb of his arousal had kept him awake and his mind had been active as he had replayed the events of the previous night.

Wearily he slid his hand from his jaw and rubbed the back of his neck. There had been some truth in Isobel's accusation that he hadn't understood how she had sought comfort from her grief in music and song writing. He had been jealous that she had turned to the company of her friends from the band, but his inability to express his own feelings about the loss of their baby meant that he had failed to support her when she had needed him.

He glanced at the photos on the wall of the Stone Ladies performing at various venues around the world. Despite the tensions in their marriage he had not expected her to leave him. Isobel had made a new life for herself, and the pictures seemed to mock him with the message that she did not need him—financially, emotionally or any other way.

But she had needed him last night, Constantin mused. It was significant that when she had escaped from the stalker, she hadn't asked the concierge to call the police, but instead had run straight to *him* for help. When he had driven her home from the party she had been adamant that their marriage was over, but after her terrifying confrontation with the stalker she had rushed into *his* arms, desperate for his protection.

The way she had responded to him when he had kissed her was further proof that she was not immune to him as she would like him to think.

Constantin's jaw hardened. His uncle's threat to hand the role of Chairman of DSE to his cousin Maurio was nothing short of blackmail, but to claim his birthright he knew he had no option but to play Alonso's game. The hard truth was that he needed to show his uncle that he was reconciled with his wife. The incident with the stalker had given him an ideal opportunity to get close to Isobel and persuade her to give their marriage another chance. Only he would know that the reconciliation would be temporary, he thought grimly.

CHAPTER SIX

MEMORIES OF THE previous evening snapped into Isobel's mind the second she opened her eyes. Amazingly, she had slept soundly and not dreamed about the stalker, but now that she was awake she remembered David's strange air of nervy excitement, which had quickly turned to anger when she had refused to go away with him.

She rolled over in bed and squinted against the bright sunshine pouring in through the open curtains, feeling puzzled because she distinctly remembered pulling them shut last night.

'I apologise for waking you.' Constantin's deep voice spoke from the doorway and Isobel's heart performed a somersault as she watched him walk towards the bed. He placed the cup of tea he had made her on the bedside table. It was unfair that even after spending the night sleeping on the sofa he still looked as if he had stepped from the pages of a glossy magazine, she thought wryly as she studied his superbly tailored light grey suit, expensive white shirt and blue tie that matched the vivid blue of his eyes.

She ran a hand through her tousled hair, feeling self-conscious that her face was scrubbed of make-up and flushed with sleep. 'That's okay. It's time I was up anyway.' The clock showed that it was nine-thirty. 'I don't usually sleep in this late.'

He shrugged. 'You had an eventful night.'

The glint in his gaze made Isobel think that he was remembering, as she was, the passion that had flared between them when he had kissed her. He could have taken her to bed last night, she acknowledged, embarrassed to recall how eagerly she had responded to him. Hell, he could have tumbled her down onto the sofa and possessed her fast and hard with no foreplay and she would have let him. But he hadn't taken what she had offered so freely, and that made his next words all the more surprising.

'I have to go to the New York office today. I would cancel, but a problem has arisen which requires my personal attention. I want you to come with me. The stalker is still at large,' he continued, predicting her question *why* before she voiced it. 'The police don't have much to go on to help them find the man, but until they do I don't think you should be alone.'

He sat down on the edge of the bed, and his nearness immediately sent Isobel's pulse-rate soaring. He had obviously taken a shower in her small bathroom, and the distinctive spicy fragrance of his aftershave teased her senses. Her breath became trapped in her throat when he lifted a strand of her hair and coiled it around his finger.

'My concern for your safety is not the only reason I would like you to accompany me to the States,' he murmured. 'How about us starting over, Isabella? Once my business is finished in New York we could spend a few days in the city and get to know each other again.'

His sexy smile was almost Isobel's undoing. Her heart had leapt at his words, and there was a part of her that desperately wanted to agree to his suggestion. But she had noticed that he did not smile with his eyes, and she sensed an air of reserve beneath his charming manner that chilled her. Something about his sudden U-turn over the divorce made her suspicious, and her voice was cool when she answered him.

'Why?'

Constantin was thrown by the question. It occurred to him that this new, more self-assured Isobel was no longer besotted with him as she had been when he had married her. If he was to stand any chance of persuading her to agree to a reconciliation he would have to be more open with her.

'I accept that many of the problems which led to us separating were due to my reluctance to talk about my feelings, and in particular about losing our baby.' He visualised Arianna, so tiny and perfect, so still and lifeless, and his heart clenched. 'As a child, I was not encouraged to show my emotions, and the habit carried through into my adult life,' he said gruffly.

Isobel bit her lip as she recalled her feeling of desolation after the miscarriage. 'Your attitude towards me changed after I lost the baby,' she said huskily. 'I couldn't get close to you, and you never wanted to talk about what had happened. I couldn't understand why. At the beginning of our marriage we were happy. We spent time together, and not only in bed,' she said quickly when his eyes glinted.

She took a steadying breath. 'Losing our baby was devastating. But things had changed—you had changed—*before* I had the miscarriage. In Italy, when we stayed at Casa Celeste, you…you were suddenly not the man I had married.'

Her mind flew to the exquisite villa on the shores of Lake Albano, close to Castel Gandolfo—the Pope's summer residence. Casa Celeste had been the De Severino family's ancestral home for four hundred years, but Constantin preferred to live in a modern penthouse apartment in the centre of Rome, or, when he was in London, the house in Grosvenor Square.

When Isobel had first visited Casa Celeste she had felt
overawed by its elegant façade, and its myriad bedrooms
and bathrooms and grand reception rooms with their sump-
tuous frescoed walls and ceilings. She had commented
that the house seemed like a museum, and Constantin had
explained that his father had been an avid collector of art
and antiques.

Studying the portrait of the previous Marchese De Severino, Isobel had seen no warmth in Constantin's father's
eyes and she had wondered what kind of parent he had been
to his only son. Constantin's tight-lipped expression when
she asked about his father made her think that they had not
been close. The wood-panelled entrance hall of Casa Celeste was lined with portraits of Constantin's aristocratic
ancestors, and Isobel had been struck by the realisation
that the child she was carrying was the next generation in
the noble lineage of the De Severino family. Looking at
the haughty faces of her baby's predecessors, she had felt
out of her depth, and she had wondered if Constantin was
secretly disappointed that the mother of his heir had been
a miner's daughter before he had made her his Marchesa.

'I had the feeling when we stayed at Casa Celeste that
you thought our marriage was a mistake. I didn't fit into
your sophisticated lifestyle and I wasn't a glamorous so-
cialite like the women you were used to. I…I sensed that
you were ashamed of me,' she said huskily.

He looked genuinely surprised. 'That's nonsense.'

'Is it? Then explain why you turned into a stranger on
that trip, and why you became cold and distant.'

Constantin frowned. 'Nothing changed. You imagined
things.'

'You slept in another bedroom—at the opposite end
of the house.'

'I moved into another room because you felt uncomfortable as your pregnancy advanced and you were too hot when we shared a bed.'

Isobel was unconvinced, especially when she remembered how well the villa's air-conditioning system worked. The only reason she'd been able to think of for why Constantin had insisted on separate bedrooms was that he had found the visible signs of her pregnancy unattractive. She had loved her rounded belly, but when she had excitedly placed Constantin's hand on her stomach so that he could feel the faint fluttering as their baby moved he had tensed and quickly stepped away from her.

His reaction had been all the more surprising because a few days before they had gone to Italy he had accompanied her to her second antenatal scan, and his hard features had softened when he had seen the image of their baby girl on the screen. Arianna had been perfectly formed and appeared to be healthy. Her little heart had been beating strongly. There had been no reason to think that her pregnancy would not continue, Isobel thought emotively, no indication of the terrible events that had followed days after she and Constantin had arrived at Casa Celeste.

'You were unsettled at the villa,' she insisted, recalling how he had seemed permanently on edge. They had gone to Italy because he had needed to attend a board meeting at DSE's head office in Rome, but in August Isobel had found the scorching temperature in the city too much, and so they had transferred to Casa Celeste, where it was cooler by the lake. The moment they had walked through the front door she had sensed a change in Constantin, and she had been puzzled by his reluctance to spend time at his childhood home.

On their first night at the villa she had been woken by him crying out in his sleep, but he had dismissed his nightmare as a result of drinking too much red wine and told her he couldn't remember what he had dreamed about. From then on he had slept in a different bedroom, but Isobel knew that his nights had been disturbed.

'You had nightmares. I heard you shouting in your sleep.'

He shrugged. 'I seem to recall that I had a dream the night we arrived. I also remember that the wine I'd drunk that evening hadn't tasted right. I suspect it had gone bad, which probably accounted for my disturbed sleep.'

'No.' Isobel held her ground. 'You had nightmares on other nights.' She shivered. 'Your cries were…ungodly—like an animal in terrible pain. You must have dreamed about something truly horrific.'

Constantin stiffened. 'How could you have heard me? My room was far away from yours and the walls of Casa Celeste are too thick for sound to carry any distance.'

'I…' She flushed, and wished she had not started the thread of conversation, but it was too late to backtrack. 'I was standing outside your bedroom door one night and I heard you shouting. Your words didn't make sense. You kept saying, "He meant to do it, he meant to kill her." I had no idea what you meant and I guessed you were dreaming.'

Constantin knew exactly what his shouts had meant and what his dream had revealed, but he had no intention of giving Isobel an explanation.

'Why did you come to my room?' His curiosity deepened as he watched rosy colour flare along her cheekbones. 'Had you felt unwell, or been concerned about the baby?' His voice became terse as a thought struck him. 'Did you have warning signs that something was wrong with your pregnancy which led to the miscarriage a few days later?'

'No…it was nothing like that.' She sighed. 'If you must know, I went to your room because I…I wanted you to make love to me.'

She glimpsed a flash of some indefinable emotion in his eyes. As his mouth curved into an arrogantly satisfied smile she fought the urge to cover her hot face with her hands. 'Why is that so surprising?' she said defensively. 'Up until that trip to Italy we had enjoyed a passionate love life.'

'Yes, you certainly disproved the theory that pregnancy can have a negative effect on a woman's libido,' he drawled.

Constantin visualised Isobel in the second trimester of her pregnancy. The morning sickness she'd suffered in the early months had disappeared and her skin had glowed, her hair had been glossy and her body had developed lush curves that he had found intensely desirable. When they had first met, their passion for one another had been mind-blowing, and to his pleasure pregnancy had heightened her enjoyment of sex.

Before the trip to Italy they had made love every night, but the return of his nightmares had been a grim reminder that he should never have got involved with her.

'I'm not ashamed to admit that I missed having sex when you decided that we should have separate bedrooms,' Isobel said tautly.

They had only slept apart at the villa for a handful of nights before she'd lost the baby, and life had never been the same again, Constantin remembered. When they had returned to London he had attempted to comfort her, but she had been inconsolable and he had told himself he deserved her rejection.

He glanced at her lovely face and her mass of honey-gold hair tumbling around her shoulders, and felt a tightening in his groin.

'Why *didn't* you come into my room when we were at Casa Celeste and tell me you wanted to make love?'

Isobel shrugged. 'I couldn't.' She did not want to admit that she had been afraid he'd been turned off by her pregnant shape and might have rejected her. 'When I realised you were having a nightmare I wondered if I should wake you, but then you stopped shouting and I thought it best not to disturb you.'

Her voice trembled. 'Two days later I lost the baby, and there was no reason for us to stay together. You told me last week that you had only married me because I was pregnant,' she reminded him. 'That's why I'm surprised by your suggestion that we could start again.'

She watched Constantin's eyes narrow, and sensed he was trying to think of a reason that would convince her to give their marriage another chance. It was lucky she had not expected him to make a declaration that he loved her, she thought drily.

'Anyway, I can't jet off to New York. I've been writing songs for the Stone Ladies' next album and I'll be working with the band in the recording studio this week.'

'Couldn't you put the recording session off until another time?'

His casual tone riled her. 'No, I can't. A lot of other people are involved, sound engineers, studio technicians. We are professional musicians,' she told him curtly. 'My career is as important to me as DSE is to you.'

Constantin struggled to hide the anger in his voice. 'I'm well aware that your career with the Stone Ladies is your top priority, but for heaven's sake, Isobel, the stalker hurt you last night when he tried to grab you. Surely you take the issue of your safety seriously?'

'Of course I do, and I appreciate your concern. But it's unnecessary. I sent a text message to Ryan last night telling him about the stalker, and he invited me to stay with him and Emily for a few days.' She glanced at the clock again. 'As a matter of fact, they'll be here at any minute to collect me. Ryan said he'll ring the doorbell twice so that I know it's him.'

Constantin felt the acid burn of jealousy in his stomach at the thought of pretty-boy Fellows rushing to Isobel's rescue like a proverbial knight in shining armour. The guitarist was engaged to his girlfriend, he reminded himself. In his mind he heard the voice of his father's second wife.

'*You are jealous of any man I happen to glance at, Franco,*' Lorena had cried.

Dio! His jealousy of Isobel's friendships with other people was proof that he was no better than his father, Constantin told himself grimly. De Severino blood ran through his veins, and it was possible that an unpredictable, violent monster lived inside him as it had in his father. The idea sickened him. It was imperative that he persuade Isobel to return to him until he had secured the chairmanship of DSE, but the reason he had deliberately drawn away from her in the first year of their marriage still remained. She was the only woman who had ever incited feelings of jealous possessiveness in him.

He visualised his father stretching a hand towards Lorena as they stood on the balcony. Seconds later she had fallen to her death. Her scream would haunt Constantin for ever.

The sound of two rings on the doorbell dragged his mind from the past. He stared at Isobel and his gut ached with a longing that was more than physical desire. However, his voice gave away nothing of his thoughts. 'The cavalry are here,' he drawled sardonically. He sauntered across the room but paused in the doorway and glanced back at her. 'Promise me you'll take care, *piccola*?'

How could Constantin sound as though he cared about

her when she knew full well that he didn't give a damn? Isobel wondered. She shrugged helplessly. 'I promise.'

'*Bene.*' His voice was soft, and his smile stole her breath. She closed her eyes while she fought for composure, and when she opened them again he had gone.

'*Jezebel!*' David's high-pitched voice shook with fury. 'I read in the newspapers that you are married. But you are *mine*, Izzy. You should not have allowed this other man to lay his hands on your body. You have betrayed me, and you must pay, *bitch…*'

Isobel's fingers trembled as she hit the button on her mobile phone to end the call, cutting off the stalker as he issued a string of obscenities. It was the first time that he had actually threatened her, but as yet the police had been unable to trace him and they were powerless to do anything to help, other than to advise her not to answer calls from a withheld number.

It was so unfair, she thought, frustrated. She felt hounded and increasingly worried. Although she had changed her mobile-phone number again, David had somehow got hold of her new number. Her heart had leapt into her throat when the message *number withheld* had flashed on her phone's screen, but out of fearful curiosity she had listened to the stalker's latest hysterical outburst.

The day after the charity fund-raising party, pictures of her and Constantin kissing on the dance floor had been in all the tabloids. The journalists must have done their homework, because the revelation that she was married to the billionaire head of the luxury goods company DSE was prominent in the gossip columns, as was speculation about the state of her current relationship with Constantin. Fortunately the Stone Ladies PR office had dealt with the press interest, but the phone calls from David had started again, and over the past few days his messages had become increasingly menacing.

'Are you sure you'll be all right while Emily and I are in the Caribbean?' Ryan strolled across the patio to where Isobel was sitting in the garden of his house in Chelsea. 'You're welcome to stay here until the police have caught the nutter responsible for the nuisance calls you've been receiving.' He shot a sharp glance at her tense expression. 'Has the stalker phoned you again? Emily won't mind if we postpone our trip.'

'I haven't heard from him,' Isobel lied. 'And I certainly don't want you to postpone your plans. I know you've been looking forward to your holiday, especially since you announced your engagement to Emily in the press. Hopefully you'll avoid the paparazzi while you're in St Lucia.'

Ryan still looked concerned. 'I don't like the idea of you going back to your flat. I'd be happier if you would go and stay with Carly and Ben.'

She shook her head. 'I'd have to tell Carly about the stalker. I don't want to cause her any stress, especially in the first crucial weeks of her pregnancy.'

Isobel had hidden the shaft of pain she'd felt when her friend had revealed that she was expecting a baby. She was truly delighted for Carly and Ben, who had already asked her to be godmother to their first child. The business with the stalker was getting out of hand, she brooded. It was bad enough that her life was disrupted, but she did not want her problems to affect her friends.

Her phone rang and she jumped like a startled deer, which spoiled her pretence that she was unconcerned by the stalker and earned her a close look from Ryan. Her eyes flew to the phone's screen and she let out a shaky breath as she recognised the number, and at the same time her heart-rate accelerated.

'Has the stalker contacted you since I spoke to you yesterday?' Constantin said without preamble, ignoring her
query about the weather in New York. 'I assume you have
told the police that David has somehow discovered your
new number and phoned you several times this week?'

'I reported his calls,' Isobel confirmed.

'Has he rung today?'

She glanced at Ryan, who was standing within earshot
of her conversation. She could hardly tell Constantin about
the stalker's recent, threatening call when she had denied
to Ryan that she had received any more nuisance calls. If
she told the truth, she knew Ryan would cancel his holiday with his fiancée.

'He hasn't phoned today,' she said with forced airiness.
'Hopefully David has got bored of his game.'

A snort of disbelief was followed by a tense silence from
the other end of the line as Constantin struggled to control
his frustration. He felt a strong urge to return to London
immediately so that he could shake some sense into Isobel. 'I don't believe the stalker is playing a game,' he said
curtly. 'I wish you would allow me to hire a bodyguard
to protect you while this man remains a potential threat.'

'You're overreacting. I don't want a bodyguard.'

He gave an exasperated sigh. 'I should have known that
you would not accept my help, but in this instance your
determination to be independent is foolish.'

Isobel's nerves were on edge following the phone call
from the stalker, and her temper flared. 'I'm not six years
old,' she reminded Constantin coldly. 'I can take care of
myself.' She winced as he swore down the phone. 'Really,
there is no need to worry about me. I'm going up to Derbyshire to visit Mum. I think she's lonely now that Dad has
gone, and while I'm away from London maybe the stalker
will lose interest in me.' Realising that she could spend all

day arguing with Constantin, she said quickly, 'I've got to go. I hope your business trip is successful,' she added in a conciliatory tone before ending the call.

The roads in central London were fairly quiet in the middle of the afternoon before the start of the rush hour. As Isobel drove past the front of her apartment building she waved to the new concierge who she had met when Ryan had accompanied her to her flat a couple of days ago to collect her post. The concierge had introduced himself as Bill. Apparently, he was ex-army and had been a champion boxer for his regiment, a statement borne out by his massive build and misshapen nose that looked as if it had been broken on several occasions.

A ramp led down to the underground car park beneath the building. She parked in her bay, slid out of the car and opened the boot to retrieve the bag she had taken with her when she had stayed with Ryan and Emily. The couple were well suited, she mused. It was wonderful to see Ryan so happy after the depression he had suffered following Simon's death.

On the other side of the car park an engine started up. Out of the corner of her eye Isobel saw a white van drive towards her, but she paid it no attention; every other vehicle in London seemed to be a white van. In her mind she planned what clothes to pack for the trip to visit her mother in Derbyshire. She closed the boot of her car and turned to walk towards the lifts, but the van was blocking her path and as the driver jumped out her heart crashed painfully against her ribcage.

'You!'

David did not reply, and his silence unnerved her more than if he had verbally abused her as he had over the phone.

He stared at her with wild eyes and when he did finally speak his tone was coldly menacing.

'You must come with me, Izzy.'

Her eyes darted to the van's open rear door and the length of rope coiled up inside. Constantin's words jerked into her mind. 'I don't believe the stalker is playing a game,' he had said seriously. Fear paralysed her, but as David suddenly lunged towards her and grabbed hold of her arms she reacted instinctively and kicked him in the shin. He yelped, but tightened his grip, his breath coming in panting rasps.

'You will be mine for all eternity. Death will unite us for ever.'

'Let me go!' She struggled frantically as he tried to force her into the back of the van. He was surprisingly strong and Isobel found she was no match for him. If only she could alert someone's attention, but there was no one in the car park and her desperate scream echoed around the underground vault.

The stalker's fingers were biting into her arms and her thin jacket offered scant protection. She renewed her efforts to escape, but he possessed a manic strength and pushed her so violently that she crumpled half inside the van. She felt sick with terror. If he managed to get her inside the van and restrained her with the rope before driving away she dreaded to imagine what he intended to do with her.

Fired by desperation, she fought like a wildcat, kicking out at him so that he swore and released her arms. David renewed his attack, but the adrenalin coursing through Isobel meant that she barely felt the blows he dealt her. Distantly she became aware of the sound of pounding footsteps, a harsh male voice shouting. Suddenly the blows from the stalker ceased and Bill the concierge's bulky figure appeared.

'Get your hands off the lady!'

With a roar of fury, David threw her into the van. Her head struck the edge of the door with such force that she felt agonising pain shoot through her skull before blackness descended.

CHAPTER SEVEN

TWENTY-FOUR HOURS after she had been attacked by the stalker, the doctor at the hospital where Isobel had been taken by ambulance explained that, following an episode of concussion, it was common to experience a moderate to severe headache.

'You were admitted overnight as a precaution. If your vision becomes blurred, or you start vomiting, you must return to hospital, but you were only unconscious for a few minutes and there should not be any lasting damage.'

Isobel nodded and winced as the slight movement hurt like mad. She wondered if the doctor would consider the pneumatic drill vibrating inside her skull was merely a moderate headache. All things considered, she knew she had got off lightly. The bruises on her arms, ribs and temple would fade and she had been assured by the medical staff that the nauseous sensation and the feeling that she wanted to burst into tears were side-effects of shock.

'I can't believe such an awful thing happened,' Carly said for probably the tenth time. 'Thank heavens the new concierge at the apartment building saw you being attacked on CCTV and rushed to your rescue. You should have told me about the stalker, Izzy.'

'I didn't want to worry you.' She gave her best friend a rueful glance. The band's keyboard player looked visibly upset, and Isobel added guilt to the list of emotions churning inside her. Ben and Carly had rushed to the hospital as soon as they had heard what had happened. The Stone Ladies' manager, Mike Jones, as well as various other friends, had also visited and expressed shock and sympathy. Ryan had phoned when he had heard about the attack, but thankfully she had managed to dissuade him from cutting short his holiday to come home. Isobel was grateful for everyone's concern, but she longed to be alone and have some peace and quiet.

She closed her eyes, but the sound of a familiar gravelly voice made her jerk them open again and her stomach dipped as she looked towards the door and met Constantin's brilliant blue gaze. For several simmering seconds it was as if they were the only two people in the universe, connected by a mystical force that defied description.

'*Dio! Isabella.*' There was a curious nuance in his tone, and Isobel was shocked by his haggard appearance. His skin was grey beneath his tan and his jacket was badly creased as if he had slept in his clothes.

'You're in New York.' She grimaced at the inanity of her statement, and told herself it was the shock of the attack, not the shock of seeing Constantin, that had scrambled her brain.

'I flew back the moment I received Carly's call.'

Isobel shot her friend a reproachful look. 'There was no need…' she began, but Constantin stalled her.

'There was every need,' he said grimly. 'I am your husband and as such your next of kin.' He did not add that when he had learned Isobel had been attacked by the stalker he could have sworn that his heart stopped beating for what had felt like a lifetime.

He came into the room and immediately dominated the small space. Isobel swallowed as he leaned over the bed and gently, so gently, traced a finger over the swelling above her left eye. A muscled flickered in his jaw.

'Thank goodness Bill got to you before you were seriously harmed.'

Her eyes widened. 'How do you know the name of the concierge at my apartment building?'

'Bill Judd is a private protection officer. You refused to allow me to hire a bodyguard to look after you so I did the next best thing and appointed Bill to watch your flat in case the stalker returned.' Constantin ignored her swift intake of breath. 'I did not know you had learned to drive while we've been separated, and Bill wasn't expecting you to park in the car park. Fortunately he kept a close eye on all the CCTV screens and was able to reach you before the stalker forced you into his van. But he was not quick enough to prevent you from being injured.'

Once again, Isobel heard a strange catch in his voice, as if he was struggling to contain his emotions. But she must have imagined it, she decided, because the one thing she knew about her enigmatic husband was that he was never troubled by strong emotions.

'Do you happen to have your passport with you?'

She gave him a puzzled look. 'It's in my handbag. I always carry it with me.'

'Good, that means it won't be necessary to stop off at your flat on the way to the airport.'

'Hold on a minute.' She lifted her head from where she had been resting it against the pillows and felt as though a red-hot poker had been thrust into her skull. 'Why do I need my passport?'

'My jet is being refuelled ready to fly us to Rome.' His eyes glittered fiercely as she opened her mouth to protest. 'Don't even think of arguing, *cara*. The stalker escaped capture. He demonstrated when he attacked you that he is disturbed and dangerous.'

Carly made a distressed sound. 'You mean he might try and hurt Izzy again?'

'H...how did he get away,' Isobel asked shakily. 'Before I was knocked out I saw the concierge...bodyguard grab hold of him.'

Constantin hesitated, reluctant to frighten Isobel more than she had already been, but he could not hide the truth from her. 'The stalker was carrying a knife. He stabbed Bill in the hand and managed to drive away. The police were immediately alerted and they found the hired van abandoned a few streets from your apartment building, but unfortunately they have been unable to locate the man yet.

'His name is David Archibald, by the way. It was possible to identify him from the CCTV film. He was employed as caretaker at the offices of the Stone Ladies' management company. He must have had access to personal files and computer records after the staff had gone home in the evening, and that's how he was able to discover your phone number and address.' Constantin sought and held Isobel's gaze. 'The man has a history of psychotic behaviour and the police believe he poses a threat to your safety.'

'Izzy, you have to go away with Constantin until the police catch this man,' Carly said fiercely. Her face was white and strained beneath her bright red curls, and the sight of a tear sliding down her cheek made Isobel hurt inside. She and Carly had been friends since nursery school and were as close as sisters.

'Don't worry, I'll take care of her,' Constantin assured Carly. His gentle tone surprised Isobel. In the past he had seemed to resent her close bond with the other members of the band.

After extracting a promise from Isobel that she would

accept Constantin's help, Ben and Carly left. 'There's no reason for me to go to Italy with you,' she told him as soon as they were alone. 'I realise it would be sensible not to return to my flat until the police find the stalker, but why can't I stay at the house in Grosvenor Square?'

'Whittaker has taken an extended period of leave to visit his niece in New Zealand. I need to be at DSE's head office to oversee a new project, and I want you in Rome with me so I can keep you safe.'

Isobel grimaced. 'You are not responsible for me. I need to be in London to work.'

'I checked with your manager. You've finished recording songs for the new album, and the Stone Ladies' next concert is not until September. In this instance I *am* responsible for you, Isabella.' Constantin's jaw clenched. 'I blame myself for the attack. The stalker only started acting aggressively after pictures of us kissing at the fund-raising party were published in the newspapers. That, together with the revelation in the press that you are my wife, was probably enough to have tipped the mentally disturbed man over the edge.'

He leaned over the bed and cupped her chin. 'I will never forgive myself for putting you in danger,' he said in a husky voice that sent a quiver of sensation down Isobel's spine. 'If I have to, I'll carry you out of here and put you on my plane.'

Constantin's eyes glittered as he studied her stark pallor and the vivid purple bruise on her brow. He'd read her medical notes and knew she had suffered bruising to her arms and torso as well as concussion caused by a blow to her head. It could have been worse. He shuddered to think what might have happened if the stalker had succeeded in kidnapping her. He had decided against telling Isobel that

David was a schizophrenic with a history of violent behaviour. 'Don't fight me, *tesorino,*' he murmured.

She ached all over and felt as if she had fought several rounds with a prize boxer. She did not have the physical or mental strength for a battle of wills with Constantin, especially when his face was so close to hers that she could count his silky black eyelashes. It was impossible to ignore the electric awareness simmering between them, impossible to prevent the slight tremble of her mouth as emotions threatened to overwhelm her.

Tears filled her eyes and she felt his warm breath whisper across her skin as he made a muffled sound in his throat before he claimed her lips in an achingly sensual kiss that touched her soul. After the terror she had experienced when the stalker had attacked her, the sense of safety and security she felt in Constantin's arms weakened her resistance and she simply opened her mouth beneath the gentle pressure of his and gave herself up to the pleasure of his kiss.

The memory of the passion that had flared between them, as well as the underlying tenderness in Constantin's kiss, stayed with Isobel as they drove to the airport and boarded his private jet. She had taken some strong painkillers for her headache and once the plane had taken off she leaned back in her seat and closed her eyes. Moments later, she opened them again when Constantin unfastened her seat belt and lifted her into his arms.

She peered at him groggily as the painkillers took effect. 'What are you doing?'

'Taking you to bed,' he told her as he carried her to the rear of the plane and into the bedroom, which was fitted with a large double bed. Other memories pushed into Isobel's mind, of the occasions when he had made love to her for the duration of the journey between London and

Rome. Despite her pounding headache she still managed to sound defiant.

'The hell you are! I agreed to go to Rome with you, but that's all.' She glared at him as he deposited her on the bed, but her treacherous heart leapt when he kicked off his shoes and stretched out next to her. 'I am not going to provide you with inflight entertainment.' She sat upright and groaned as pain shot through her head.

'Relax,' Constantin drawled, and pushed her gently back down onto the pillows. 'I haven't slept in thirty-six hours. When I received a phone call from Carly to tell me what had happened to you, I was…extremely concerned.' He could not begin to describe his mixture of fear for her well-being, and fury with her attacker, not to mention anger with himself that he might have triggered the stalker's aggression by kissing Isobel in public. 'I'm beat. When I make love to you I intend to be wide awake and fully energised.'

Isobel frowned as the meaning of his words penetrated the sleepy haze fogging her mind. 'Don't you mean *if*, not, *when*?'

He raised a lazy eyebrow. 'We both know that I could have hot and very satisfying sex with you any time I choose, *mia bella*,' he drawled. 'But I'm content to wait until you are ready to accept that I'm the only man who can blow your mind.'

Temper gave her the energy to snatch up a pillow and thump him with it. 'Your ego is *enormous*!'

His rich laughter echoed around the bedroom as he tugged the pillow out of her hand and pulled her down so that her head rested on his chest. He curled his arms around her, trapping her against his strong body. 'It's not the only enormous thing about me,' he whispered wickedly.

Despite herself, Isobel's lips twitched. In the early days

of their marriage Constantin had often teased her and made her laugh. They had laughed together, had fun together. What had happened to them? she wondered. Everything had started to go wrong when they had visited his ancestral home Casa Celeste and her charming, laughing husband had turned into a cold stranger.

Constantin's Roman home was a stunning penthouse apartment in the heart of the city overlooking the Piazza Navona and its famous fountains. From the outside the property was a magnificent historical building, which had been exquisitely restored by a famous Italian architect. Inside, however, the décor was ultra-modern, with huge open-plan rooms lined with glass walls that offered spectacular views across Rome.

Isobel had first visited the apartment when Constantin had invited her to spend a weekend with him. Boarding his private jet for the flight to Italy, she had noticed the glamorous stewardess glance at her cheap clothes and she had felt self-conscious that she was a lowly office assistant and her billionaire boss was in a different league. When they had arrived at the penthouse she had been overwhelmed by the luxurious surroundings and even more overwhelmed by Constantin. He had been utterly charming as he had dispelled her shyness as quickly as he had dispensed with her clothes, and, soon after, her virginity.

Now, as she walked through the apartment, Isobel felt a sense of sadness for the innocent girl of three years ago who had been swept off her feet and fallen irrevocably in love with her Italian lover. How naïve she had been to believe that Constantin had returned her feelings. The ugly truth was that she had been just another notch on his bedpost until he had discovered that she was carrying his heir. Her pregnancy had prompted him to marry her, but she'd never been comfortable with her title of Marchesa De Severino. She had felt like an imposter among his aristocratic friends, and after she had lost their baby she had felt like a fraud.

She assured herself that she was relieved when Constantin showed her to one of the guest bedrooms rather than the master suite. His taunt on the plane that he could take her to bed whenever he chose was not something she wanted to put to the test.

'I kept the clothes you left behind two years ago,' he said, opening a wardrobe to reveal a rail full of elegant designer outfits that she had worn on the occasions when she had accompanied him to glamorous social events.

At least she would not have to immediately go shopping, Isobel thought. All she'd brought with her from England was the bag containing a few items of clothes and makeup that she'd taken to Ryan's and she'd had with her when the stalker had attacked her.

Her eyes were drawn to the vase of yellow roses on the dressing table. Following her gaze, Constantin explained, 'I asked the housekeeper to put yellow roses in your room because I know they are your favourite flowers.'

Isobel recalled that when they had returned from their honeymoon he had filled the house in London with yellow roses and her foolish heart had leapt as she'd taken the gesture as a sign that he cared for her.

'You remembered,' she whispered, feeling a sudden rush of tears to her eyes. Needing time to regain her composure, she leaned forwards to inhale the roses' heady perfume. 'They're beautiful. Thank you.'

He grimaced. 'Perhaps I should not have told you of my involvement, knowing how you dislike accepting anything from me. No doubt you'll consign the roses to the rubbish bin.'

She was startled by the bitterness in his voice. 'What do you mean?'

'You left every single gift that I'd given you behind when you abandoned our marriage, including the diamond necklace I gave you for a birthday present.'

She pictured the exquisite pear-drop diamond pendant that he had fastened around her neck on the evening of her birthday, when they had been about to host a dinner party for some of Constantin's business associates. Isobel would have preferred to celebrate her birthday quietly, maybe dinner at a country pub, but he had insisted on holding a lavish dinner in her honour.

'Only the finest quality diamonds will do for my wife,' Constantin had told her as she'd stared in the mirror at the glittering necklace that had felt cold and hard against her skin. His words had made her feel cold inside as she'd wondered if he had given her the necklace to make a statement of his wealth.

'The necklace must have cost thousands of pounds. I didn't feel comfortable wearing something so valuable.'

'Why don't you be honest, and say you didn't want the necklace or the other items of jewellery and the clothes I bought you because, although you were happy to accept birthday presents from your friends, you hated accepting anything from me?' Constantin growled. 'You accused me of being distant, but when I tried to bridge the gap between us you pushed me away.'

'I didn't want presents, I wanted…' Isobel broke off, frustrated that she could not make him understand that she hadn't been interested in material things. What she had longed for was for him to share himself with her, to open up his thoughts and emotions that he kept locked away. 'I wanted you to take an interest in me as a person,' she muttered. 'I wanted our marriage to be an equal partnership, but you seemed to think that if you gave me expensive presents I should be content, and not want anything else such as to see my friends or pursue my music career.' Her resentment and unhappiness had increased until the only answer had been for her to leave him.

'Everything had to be your way, Constantin,' she accused him bitterly. 'My hopes and dreams didn't count. You reminded me of my father. My mother was a wonderful pianist, and years ago she had the chance to play professionally with an orchestra, but Dad persuaded her that she wasn't good enough. He said she should carry on working as a piano teacher and not give up her job for a silly dream.'

'In our case, there was no need for you to work,' Constantin said curtly. 'I provided you with a good lifestyle.'

Isobel sucked in a breath, trying to control her temper. 'That statement shows just how little you understood me. I didn't want to be provided for. It was, *is,* important for me to work and provide for myself, to feel independent...'

'Your desire for independence did nothing to help our marriage.'

'Our marriage was beyond help. After we lost our baby there was nothing to hold us together.'

Her throat suddenly ached. 'Constantin...' She swung round to face him and thought she glimpsed hurt in his eyes, but his lashes swept down and hid his emotions. 'I admit I felt uncomfortable when you gave me expensive gifts. I felt like a...a charity case, like Cinderella. I was the penniless secretary, who landed herself a billionaire husband,' she reminded him. She bit her lip.

'When we announced our engagement, your PA, Julie, made a snide remark in front of many people in the office that I was a gold-digger and I must have deliberately engineered falling pregnant with your baby so that you would marry me.'

'Why did you care what my PA said? You knew as well as I did that it was my fault you conceived,' he said curtly. 'You had told me on the weekend we spent together here that you were not on the pill. Contraception was my responsibility, but I wasn't as careful as I should have been.'

Isobel felt her face grow warm as she recalled the occasion Constantin had made love to her in the shower. Their scorching desire had been as uncontrollable as a wildfire, and she had only remembered that he hadn't used protection that one time when she had stared at the blue line on the pregnancy test and felt sick with worry at the prospect of telling her father that she was going to be a single mother.

'Why did it matter what anyone else thought about our relationship?' he demanded.

'Julie was right when she guessed that you only married me because I was expecting your baby. When she said those things in the office, I felt humiliated,' Isobel said in a low voice. 'For most of my childhood my father was out of work. It wasn't his fault. He was injured in an accident in the coal mine, but the pit was closed down and he didn't receive the compensation he was owed. There was a shortage of jobs where we lived, and Dad's injuries limited the type of work he could do, so the family survived on his unemployment benefit. Mum earned a small income from teaching piano lessons, but I know my parents struggled to make ends meet.'

She sighed. 'Kids at school can be cruel. I wasn't the only one who was taunted for being a scrounger. That was the name the pupils from better-off families called those of us whose families depended on social welfare payments. I felt ashamed that my family lived on handouts, and when

I left school I vowed that I would always work and be independent. I guess it was a pride thing, but I was determined never to accept anything from anyone.'

'Surely that did not include gifts from your husband?' Constantin said harshly. 'I enjoyed buying you things. It gave me pleasure to see you dressed in beautiful clothes, and I chose pieces of jewellery that I thought would suit you and because I hoped they would give you pleasure. But instead you acted as if I had insulted you.'

'I didn't want you to think I had married you for your money.' She glanced at him and saw incomprehension in his eyes. 'I didn't belong in your world,' she said huskily.

'You might have believed that, but I certainly didn't.' Constantin frowned, trying to absorb what Isobel had told him about herself. She had clearly been deeply affected by her childhood and her family's financial situation, but he had been unaware that she felt sensitive of other people's opinion that she had married him because he was wealthy. Of the many women he had met who deserved the label gold-digger, Isobel was definitely not one of them.

'How is your headache?' he asked abruptly.

'Completely gone. The couple of hours that I slept on the plane worked wonders.'

'If you feel up to it, we'll go out for dinner.' He strode across the room and glanced back at her from the doorway. It was early evening, and the sun sinking below the horizon emitted golden rays that streamed through the window and gilded her slender frame. 'I never thought you married me for financial gain, Isabella,' he said gruffly. He hesitated. 'And, contrary to what I told you when you came to see me in London a few weeks ago, I did not marry you only because you were carrying my child.'

Isobel was stunned into silence by Constantin's enigmatic statement, and as she watched him walk out of the room she wondered if she dared to believe him.

CHAPTER EIGHT

'TRATTORIA PEPE!' ISOBEL smiled as she recognised the charming trattoria tucked in a corner of a small piazza, which was rarely discovered by tourists. Constantin had shown her many of Rome's hidden gems when they had lived together, and the trattoria had been their favourite place to eat traditional, expertly prepared Roman food. 'You brought me here the first time I visited Rome.'

'Pepe's signature dish of *porchetta* served with herbs, olives and mozzarella is still the best dish you'll find in all of Rome, in my opinion,' Constantin said as he ushered her inside the tiny restaurant.

They were welcomed by Pepe himself, and the trattoria's owner greeted Isobel like a long-lost relative, kissing her on both cheeks as he spoke to her mainly in Italian, with the odd English word thrown in.

'*Sono lieto di incontrarvi di nuovo.* I am happy to meet you again,' she replied, when Pepe finally paused to draw a breath. The conversation continued for several minutes before the trattoria's patron and head chef hurried back to his kitchen.

A young, good-looking waiter came to take their order and flirted outrageously with Isobel, until he saw the warning gleam in Constantin's eyes and beat a hasty retreat.

'I'm impressed by your fluency in Italian,' he told Isobel drily when they were alone.

She shrugged. 'It seemed a shame not to continue the lessons that I'd started when we were together.' When she had married Constantin, she had been keen to learn his language, aware that he wanted to bring their child up to speak Italian. But there had not been a baby, she thought painfully, and soon she would no longer be his wife.

The waiter returned with their first course and gave Isobel a lingering look, before a terse word from Constantin sent him scurrying away.

She frowned. 'Why were you rude to the waiter? He was just being friendly.'

'If he had been any *friendlier*, he would have made love to you on the table.' Constantin's jaw hardened as he struggled to control the hot rush of possessiveness that had swept through him when the waiter had smiled at Isobel. He had felt a burning desire to rearrange the waiter's handsome features with his fist. 'We might get served quicker if you refrain from flirting with the restaurant staff,' he growled.

'I wasn't flirting with the waiter.' Isobel's temper simmered. 'You're being ridiculous.'

Constantin took a long sip of wine. 'It's not surprising that you command attention from other men. You are very beautiful.' He leaned back in his chair and subjected her to a slow appraisal, noting the glossy sheen of her long blonde hair and the sensual shape of her mouth. 'But it's not only your looks that make you noticeable. It's something more than that. You were beautiful when I met you three years ago but you were painfully shy. You blushed every time I spoke to you,' he said softly, 'whereas now you have an air of self-confidence that most men would find undeniably attractive.'

Did he include himself with most men? Isobel wondered. 'I have grown more confident.' She gave him a wry smile. 'It was something of a necessity to overcome my shyness when the band became successful and I had to sing in front of huge audiences.' She chased a prawn around her plate with her fork, remembering the first time Constantin had brought her to the trattoria she had been so nervous that she had clumsily knocked over her glass of wine.

'When I first met you, I was a nobody, just an ordinary office assistant who dreamed of making it as a singer but never really believed it would happen. When I fell pregnant, my hopes and plans for the future were centred on being a mother to our baby and nothing else seemed as important.' A shadow of pain crossed her expressive face. 'But after we lost Arianna, I felt…irrelevant. I wasn't a mother and I sensed from the widening gap between us that I didn't live up to your expectations of a good wife.'

She shook her head when he looked as though he was going to argue. 'We both know that our marriage wasn't working. I guess we dealt with our grief about the baby in different ways. I wanted to talk about Arianna but you withdrew into yourself, and I had no idea what you were thinking…or feeling.'

'So you turned to your friends who you had known since you were a child,' Constantin said heavily. In his heart, he knew he had not been able to give her the support she had needed from him. He had shied away from acknowledging the pain of losing their baby. It had been easier to lock his emotions away and ignore them—just as he had done as a young boy when his mother had died—but in doing that he had also ignored Isobel's need for them to grieve together for Arianna.

'I poured my feelings into the songs I wrote, and found some small comfort playing the piano and creating music.

When I'd moved to London from Derbyshire with the rest of the band, we played gigs in pubs, but I stopped performing after I married you. I hadn't thought about the band becoming successful when we started performing again, it was just something to take my mind off the miscarriage. But to my amazement the Stone Ladies were spotted by a record producer and everything quickly escalated.'

She leaned across the table and trapped Constantin's gaze. 'When the Stone Ladies were offered a record contract it was a chance for all of us in the band to have the music career that we had longed for since we were teenagers. My father had told me I was a fool to chase a dream, but the dream was coming true. I had an opportunity to be someone in my own right, not a daughter, or a wife, but *me,* a girl from nowhere who was suddenly a serious musician earning more money that I'd ever imagined.'

Constantin frowned. 'You were married to a billionaire and did not need to earn money.'

'*Yes, I did,*' Isobel said fiercely. 'It was important to me to make my own way in the world. On our wedding day, at the reception, I overheard a comment from one of the guests that I had landed myself a meal ticket for life.'

The memory of that excruciating moment still made Isobel shudder. The catty remark had been made by Contessa Ghislaine Montenocci, a member of the Italian nobility who looked down her thin, aristocratic nose at anyone who did not have a title. 'I felt embarrassed, like I'd felt when the kids at school called my family scroungers because my father claimed unemployment benefit.

'Being a professional singer gave me a sense of pride.' Her voice became husky. 'I wanted to make my father proud of me, although I'm not sure he ever was. I...I also hoped that you might be more interested in me if I had a successful career,' she admitted. 'The women we met at social events, the wives of your friends, were all sophisticated and well educated,' she explained when he looked surprised. 'I felt I couldn't compete with them.'

'I never wanted you to compete with them,' Constantin said tersely. 'I was happy with you the way you were.'

'If that was true, why did you become so cold towards me? The truth is that you didn't feel proud of me as your wife, and no amount of designer dresses or expensive jewellery could turn me into a glamorous *marchesa*.'

Isobel stared at Constantin's chiselled features and felt frustrated that she could not make him understand. 'You told me once that your appointment as CEO of De Severino Eccellenza, and your success in driving the company forwards and making it one of Italy's highest earning businesses, was your greatest achievement.' She sighed. 'Being part of a successful band is *my* greatest achievement. But my career was one of the things that drove us apart.'

A nerve jumped in his jaw. 'We weren't driven apart. *You* walked out.'

Isobel tore her eyes from the angry gleam in his and looked down at her half-eaten dinner. Suddenly she had lost her appetite, and it seemed that Constantin was no longer hungry because he called the waiter over and requested the bill.

They walked back to the penthouse in silence, both of them lost in their private thoughts. Isobel's statement that her singing career had given her a sense of self-worth had touched a chord in Constantin. DSE's increased profits, and the fact that the company had become a globally recognised brand name since he had taken over as CEO, were the two things in his life that he felt proud of.

The trauma of witnessing his father and stepmother's fatal accident, and the terrible suspicion that Franco might have been responsible for the tragedy, haunted Constantin.

Since that dreadful day, he had avoided relationships that demanded his emotional involvement and instead focused his energy and passion on the company.

But his uncle Alonso was threatening to award the chairmanship of DSE to his gutless cousin Maurio.

It would make all his hard work over the past decade a waste of time, Constantin thought savagely. The company would not last five minutes with Maurio in charge. When he had asked Isobel to give their marriage another chance his sole aim had been to convince his uncle to appoint him Chairman. He glanced at her walking beside him, and his jaw tensed as he noted the admiring looks she attracted from every red-blooded male they passed. Somewhere along the line his priorities had changed, he acknowledged.

Isobel looked up at the full moon suspended like a huge silver disc in an indigo sky. The night air was warm and the bars and street cafés were busy. It was the first time in months that she had walked down a street without glancing over her shoulder and wondering if the stalker was watching her. The police still hadn't caught David, but she felt able to relax while she was in Rome with Constantin.

Although she did not feel very relaxed as he curved his arm around her waist when they walked past a group of young men. The close contact with his body sent molten heat surging through her veins, and memories of happier times they had shared tugged on her heart. When they had stayed in Rome soon after they were married he had taken her to dinner at Pepe's, and on the way home he had paused at every street corner to kiss her. By the time they had reached the apartment they'd been so hot for one another that they had only made it as far as the nearest sofa, she remembered.

Her face grew warm as she visualised him stripping

her naked and pushing her back against the cushions, slipping his hand between her thighs to find her wet and ready for him. She had *always* been ready for him, she thought ruefully.

'Would you like a nightcap?' he enquired as they entered the penthouse.

'No, thanks. I think I'll go straight to bed.' Isobel could not meet his gaze when her mind was full of images of him making love to her. 'Hopefully we'll hear from the British police tomorrow that they have caught the stalker. I'll be able to go home, and once the divorce is finalised we will be free of each other.'

Constantin's eyes narrowed. 'Is that really what you wish for, Isabella?'

'Yes.' Emotion choked her voice. Dinner at Pepe's had been a poignant reminder of everything she had lost, everything that might have been. 'I admit I had wondered if perhaps there was a chance we could get back together, but our conversation tonight proved that our differences are too great.'

She did not trust herself to continue and turned away from him before he saw the tears she was trying to hold back. 'It's like you said, Constantin. There's no point dwelling on the past. We need to move forwards, in our case, *on separate paths*.'

Constantin stood in front of the sliding glass doors in his bedroom, which led outside to a balcony that ran the length of penthouse and overlooked the piazza. Not that he ever ventured onto the balcony, but the view across the city even through the pane of glass was spectacular. Tonight, however, as he nursed a crystal tumbler of single malt, he barely registered Rome's famous historical skyline. Instead his thoughts were focused on his wife, who was occupying the guest room next door to his suite.

It was happening again. He had spent less than twenty-four hours in her company and already his resolve to keep his distance from her was under threat. He swallowed a mouthful of whisky and seriously contemplated drinking the entire bottle in the hope that it would dull the ache in his gut.

It was her smile that did it, he brooded. When Isobel smiled her whole face lit up—like when she'd recognised Pepe's Trattoria, and when she'd noticed the yellow roses in her room. She was the only woman he knew who would prefer to be given roses than diamonds.

He frowned as he recalled her telling him that her father had been out of work for much of her childhood and the family had been dependent on social welfare. Finally he understood why she was so fiercely independent. She had said that her career with the Stone Ladies had given her a sense of pride, but he had believed that she had left him because she was in love with the band's guitarist Ryan Fellows.

Jealousy was a poisonous emotion, he thought grimly. It festered in your soul like a vile worm. It was a shameful secret that he was determined to keep hidden from Isobel. For her safety he *must* control the green-eyed monster that he was convinced he had inherited from his father. *Dio*, tonight at the restaurant he had wanted to *kill* the young waiter who had flirted with her.

Was that how his father had felt when his beautiful young wife had smiled at other men?

Constantin pictured his stepmother's laughing face. He saw her tossing her hair and leaning forwards so that her breasts almost fell out of her tiny bikini top. *Be an angel and put sun cream on my back, Con, sweetie.*

He had gone home to Casa Celeste for the school holidays and had spent all summer having erotic fantasies about his stepmother. His father had noticed him following Lorena around like a lovesick puppy and there had been a huge row. He had never seen Franco as angry as he had been that day. Later, he had heard his father and Lorena arguing on the balcony.

Santa Madonna! Would the images in his mind ever fade? He finished his drink, but as he was about to turn away from the window a movement outside caught his attention. Isobel had stepped onto the balcony, and Constantin was transfixed as the breeze moulded her long white silk nightgown against her slender body. In the moonlight she was ethereal and so very lovely that the ache inside him intensified.

For her sake he had to ignore the hot throb of desire that skewered his insides, he reminded himself. But despite his good intentions he could not stop looking at her. She had her back to him and his eyes lingered on the twin curves of her bottom beneath her silky gown. As he watched she leaned further forwards over the balcony railing.

A vision from the past flashed into his mind. His stepmother leaning over the balcony rail; falling, falling... Lorena's scream echoed inside his head.

'Get away from there!' The calm of the velvet night air was shattered by Constantin's loud shout. Startled, Isobel looked round, and gave a cry of fright when he clamped his hands around her waist like a vice and lifted her off her feet, bundling her through the sliding glass doors into his bedroom.

'What are you *doing*?'

'What am *I* doing? *Mio Dio*, what were *you* doing leaning over the railing like that?' He swore savagely and raked his hair back from his brow with a hand that was actually shaking, Isobel noticed. He was grey beneath his tan, and the expression in his eyes was like none she had ever seen before. For a few seconds she saw stark terror in his eyes before he swung away from her, poured whisky from the bottle into a glass and gulped it down.

'I was trying to get a better view of the fountains. Constantin...I was quite safe. The balcony rail is too high for me to have fallen over.'

He slowly turned back to her, and she was relieved to see he had regained some colour in his face. To her surprise, he looked almost embarrassed by his strange behaviour.

'I guess I overreacted,' he muttered. 'It's just that I hate heights.'

Her eyebrows rose. 'You hate heights, yet you live in a penthouse with a balcony.' She compressed her lips in an unsuccessful attempt to disguise their betraying quiver.

'It's not funny,' he snapped.

'Oh, come on, Constantin, it is a bit,' Isobel giggled. Her shock when he had grabbed hold of her and hauled her in off the balcony—coming so soon after the shock of being attacked by the stalker—had left her feeling slightly crazy. 'You must have one of the best views of Rome but you're too scared to enjoy it.' She gave a peal of laughter. 'It's the most human reaction you've ever shown.'

Constantin closed his eyes and tried to block out the memories that swirled like black storm clouds in his brain. It was no good. He could not prevent the film reel in his mind from playing.

He was seventeen and spending the summer at Casa Celeste. He saw his father and Franco's young, pretty second wife standing on the balcony at the top of the tower. He heard his father's harsh voice and Lorena's high-pitched tones. Standing below in the courtyard, Constantin had

*realised they were arguing again. For years afterwards
he had been unable to remember who had moved first—
his father, or Lorena. His heart had crashed with fear as
he saw Lorena topple over the balcony railing and fall
through the air. He would never forget the sound of her
scream. Moments later he had watched his father fall after
Lorena. Everything seemed to happen in slow motion but
it must have only been seconds before he heard two thuds.
Thankfully he had closed his eyes at the moment of impact. For years he had blanked out the details of what he
had witnessed—until his nightmares had revealed exactly
what had taken place on the balcony.*

He jerked his eyes open and saw Isobel staring at him.
She had teased him for being scared of heights, but she
had no idea of the stark terror that had seized him when
he had seen her lean over the balcony.

'Surely not, *cara*,' he said grittily. 'I have never failed
to react like a normal human male when I'm with you.'

Isobel belatedly realised that he was furious with her for
teasing him. Remembering the strained look on his face
when he had rushed onto the balcony, she acknowledged
that her amusement had been misplaced.

'I'm sorry,' she muttered. But her apology was also
too late. The glitter in Constantin's eyes warned her that
she had pushed him beyond his limit. But while her brain
urged her to run from his room, her limbs refused to obey.
The atmosphere between them trembled with tension that
built, second by simmering second, until it was an explosive force.

He swore as he caught hold of her and dragged her towards him. 'It will be my pleasure to demonstrate that I
have all the normal human reactions, *mia bella*,' he told her
harshly. Without giving her a chance to reply, he brought his
mouth down on hers and kissed her with savage possession.

Constantin slid his hands down and clasped Isobel's bottom in a statement of bold intent. She felt the heat of his touch brand her through her thin nightgown and she gasped as he dragged her hard against him, forcing her pelvis into contact with the solid length of his arousal. He gave her no opportunity to voice her objection as he plundered her mouth and stole his pleasure, thrusting his tongue between her lips and exploring her with a flagrant eroticism that turned her bones to liquid.

The fire had been building all evening. Long before that, she conceded, remembering the electricity that had sizzled between them when she had watched him working out in the gym at his London home. Their hunger for each other had always been a driving force in their relationship, and however much her common sense told her to stop the madness her body recognised its master and was a willing slave to the delicious sensations he was creating with his hands and mouth.

He trailed his lips down her throat, each kiss sending a little shockwave through her that made every nerve-ending tingle. She arched her neck and gave herself up to hedonistic pleasure that intensified when he drew the straps of her gown over her shoulders and peeled the sheer silk away from her breasts.

She knew she should stop him, but the realisation that she was playing into his hands was driven from her mind when he cupped her breasts in his palms and kneaded them gently. It felt so good, but good became unbelievably wonderful as he flicked his thumb pads across her nipples, sending starbursts of sensation from her breasts down to her pelvis. The ache there grew to a desperate need that made her press her hips to his so that the hard bulge beneath his trousers rubbed against the hidden sweet spot at the heart of her femininity.

He growled something against her mouth and with one fluid motion yanked her nightgown over her hips and it slithered to the floor, leaving her naked to his glittering gaze. She made a little murmur of embarrassment as he slid his hand between her legs and gave her a mocking smile when he parted her and discovered the moist heat of her arousal.

'It appears that your human reactions work well too, *tesorino*.'

She closed her eyes to block out his cynical expression. 'Constantin—*don't*!' Taunting her about her weakness for him was bad enough, but his casual use of the endearment that she had once hoped meant that he cared for her was heartbreaking.

He caught hold of her chin and tilted her head up. 'Tears, Isabella?' An expression of pain flitted across his hard-boned face. She looked fragile and achingly vulnerable, the bruises on her arms a grim reminder of her narrow escape from the mentally disturbed stalker who had become obsessed with her. 'Do you honestly believe I would hurt you?'

Isobel recalled his stark expression when he had leaned over her hospital bed. *I will never forgive myself for putting you in danger*, he'd told her with a roughness in his tone that she had never heard before.

She shook her head. 'I know you were trying to protect me when you saw me on the balcony.' She met his gaze, her clear hazel eyes containing a breathtaking honesty. 'I know I'm safe with you.'

Santa Madre! He did not want to go there. He did not want to think of the past and all its secrets. What he wanted, needed, was to lose himself in the sweet seduction of Isobel's body. To kiss her and have her kiss him back, to caress her silken skin and feel her gentle hands on his body as she stroked his own aching body and brought him to the edge of ecstasy. He would take her with him on that tumultuous ride for they shared a passion that he had never experienced as intensely with any other woman.

Isobel gave a broken sigh as Constantin claimed her mouth once more, but this time his passion was tempered by a beguiling tenderness that shattered her soul. He was *everything*. The love of her life. The two years they had been apart had been unendingly lonely. She had thousands of fans around the world and sang in front of vast audiences, but every night she had slept alone and her heart had ached for one man.

He traced his lips over the fragile line of her collarbone and made a muffled sound almost as if he were in pain as he kissed each black bruise on her arms. A shiver of pleasure feathered down Isobel's spine as he moved lower to caress her breasts, painting moist circles around each aureole before he suckled her nipples in turn while she closed her eyes and gave herself totally to his sensual magic.

Reality faded, and was replaced with a new reality where only she and Constantin existed. She felt the mattress dip when he laid her on the bed. She watched him strip, and her heart beat faster as she studied every olive-skinned, muscle-packed inch of his body. He was a work of art, but unlike Bernini's incredible sculptures on the Fountain of the Four Rivers down in the *piazza*, his skin was warm beneath her fingertips and the wiry black hairs that covered his chest and arrowed over his flat stomach and thighs were faintly abrasive against her palms.

The jutting length of his arousal was further proof, as if she needed it, that hot red blood ran through his veins. She had forgotten just how powerfully he was built and her hesitation much have shown in her eyes because he smiled crookedly as he stretched out next to her and drew her into his arms.

'Are you having second thoughts, *tesorino*?' he murmured.

And third and fourth thoughts, if he but knew it. She gave him a shaky smile. 'Two years is a long time…and I'm out of practice.'

His eyes darkened. 'There has been no one else?'

She would not lie to him. 'No.'

'Not for me, either.'

Now she was shocked. 'You mean you haven't…in *two* years?'

'We were living apart but you were, *are*, my wife.'

No wonder he was so hugely aroused, whispered a little voice in her head. Her husband was a highly sexed male and frustration must have had him climbing the walls.

He had the uncanny knack of being able to read her mind. 'Believe it,' he said drily.

Their eyes met, and the sultry promise in his focused her mind on what he was doing with his hands as he trailed a path of fire down to the cluster of golden curls at the apex of her thighs. Despite the passing of time he had total recall of how to please her, knew the exact moment when she needed him to slide one finger into her, then two, and move them in a relentless dance until she gave a husky cry of delight and desperation.

He loved that she was so unguarded in her response to him. Aware that he was about to explode, Constantin felt his iron control shatter, and with a groan he pulled her beneath him, slid his hands beneath her bottom and drove into her with a powerful thrust that brought a gasp from her.

'*Dio*, did I hurt you?' Remorse thickened his voice, but

as he made to withdraw she wrapped her long legs around his hips.

'No. It just feels so good.' Her shy smile reminded him of the first time he had made love to her, when her guileless enjoyment had made him come much faster than he had intended.

He focused entirely on giving her pleasure as he began to move, slowly at first, with strong, measured strokes that heightened their mutual excitement. She quickly learned his rhythm, lifting her hips to meet each powerful thrust. Their bodies moved in perfect accord, riding a sensual roller coaster that gathered speed—faster, faster, hurtling them towards the highest peak and hovering there for timeless moments before they crashed and burned in the climatic explosion of their simultaneous release.

A long time afterwards, Constantin rolled onto his back and immediately curled his arm around her and cradled her against his chest. The steady thud of his heartbeat beneath her ear soothed the knot of apprehension in Isobel's stomach. They needed to talk, and she was no longer sure what she hoped the outcome of the conversation would be. Had making love to her meant something to him, or was it simply to slake his sexual frustration?

'Constantin...?'

'Sleep now, *tesorino*,' he murmured. Was it her imagination, or did she sense that he was reluctant to break the languorous haze? The drift of his fingertips along her spine was hypnotic and she closed her mind to everything but the pleasure of simply being with him in the private world they had created.

Isobel had no concept of how long she'd slept, when something, a sound, woke her. Surfacing from the fog of sleep, she realised that she had heard a voice shouting. Her memory returned.

She'd had sex with Constantin last night.

Why did things never seem such a good idea the next morning?

Pale grey light slivered through the blinds, and she saw on the clock that it was four a.m. Constantin was sitting up in bed, breathing hard, as if he had run a marathon. She put her hand on his shoulder and he jumped as if he had been shot.

'*Dio!* Isobel—' he took a gulp of air '—I didn't realise you were awake.'

'I heard a noise.' Her brow wrinkled as a memory pushed up from her subconscious. 'Why were you shouting?'

'I knocked over the damned water jug. I'm sorry, *cara*, I didn't realise I'd cursed so loudly.'

She looked at him doubtfully, not quite believing his explanation. 'I thought I heard you say, "He meant to kill her," or…or something like that.' She had a vague recollection of hearing those curious words some time in the past. 'Do you still suffer from nightmares like you did two years ago at Casa Celeste?' She wished it were light enough for her to be able to see his face clearly. She looked over at his bedside table and felt even more puzzled when she made out the water jug standing upright.

'I think *you* must have been dreaming.' His breathing had slowed to a normal rate and he sounded amused.

Isobel frowned. 'I'm sure I wasn't.' It was becoming harder to think when he was nuzzling her neck. She tried to push him away but her hand somehow crept up to his shoulder as he trailed soft kisses down her throat and the slopes of her breasts. Her nipples were ultra-sensitive from his earlier caresses, and she caught her breath as he anointed each tender pink tip with his tongue.

'Constantin…' She fought the swift rush of desire that swept through her, trying to focus on the reason why he had called out. One of them had been dreaming, and she was certain it wasn't her. But his hand was between her legs, and a little moan escaped her as he unerringly found her clitoris and with skilful fingers took her swiftly to a place where only exquisite sensation existed. When he bent his dark head and replaced his fingers with his mouth, she instinctively arched her hips and quivered like a slender bow under intolerable tension before she experienced the sweet ecstasy of release. But hazily, in the back of her mind, was the thought that he had deliberately set out to distract her.

As the cool grey of pre-dawn turned to iridescent shades of pink and palest gold Constantin watched the hands on the clock move unhurriedly towards six a.m. From outside the window he could hear the pigeons cooing, the faint rumble of traffic that would grow louder as the Eternal City woke to a new day.

There was no chance he could fall back to sleep now, thank goodness. But his nightmare had been so vivid that he broke out in a cold sweat as he recalled the details. He had dreamed of two figures standing on a balcony. Not the balcony of the tower at Casa Celeste, but here at the penthouse. And the figures were not his father and Lorena, but *him* and Isobel.

She was tossing her hair, laughing as she teased him that she preferred the handsome waiter at the restaurant to him. *Basta!* Her taunts filled him with rage. *Violent rage— seething up inside him like boiling lava inside a volcano.* He reached out his hand…and then she was falling, falling. *Mio Dio!* It was just a dream, Constantin told himself.

It did not mean anything. He turned his head and stared at Isobel's face on the pillow beside him. She was so beautiful. His gut clenched. He shouldn't have brought her to Rome. He had wanted to protect her while the stalker was still at large, but perhaps his dream was a warning that she was in as much danger from *him*.

CHAPTER NINE

Isobel moved away from a group of noisy tourists outside the Church of Sant'Agnese in Agone and held her phone closer to her ear. 'I'm sorry, I didn't catch that.'

'I said, do you remember that we've been invited to the Bonuccis' party tonight, to celebrate the opening of their new hotel?'

Constantin's sexy voice made her toes curl, and she took a steadying breath before replying. 'I haven't forgotten,' she said drily. She had been in Rome for a week, and tonight's party would be the fifth social event that she and Constantin had attended. They barely spent any time alone, she reflected. He worked all day and returned home late, just in time to shower and change before they went out for the evening. It was always past midnight before they arrived back at the penthouse and Constantin invariably seemed to have a reason not to come straight to bed until she had fallen asleep.

It would be easy to think that he was trying to avoid her. That was what the insecure Isobel from two years ago would have believed, she acknowledged ruefully. But she was older, and hopefully wiser, and instead of leaping to conclusions she reminded herself that Constantin was the CEO of one of Italy's most prominent businesses and socialising and networking were part of his job.

'You should receive a delivery today.' Over the phone line she heard him hesitate. 'I bought you a dress to wear tonight.'

'It's already been delivered, and it's beautiful, thank you.'

'You don't mind?'

She sensed his surprise. In the past she had always been uptight when he'd bought her presents, and although she had politely thanked him her words had been stilted. It was little wonder that he'd felt rebuffed by her, Isobel brooded.

'I'm glad you like it,' Constantin told her. 'I saw the dress on display in a shop window and immediately knew it would suit you.'

'If you're home in time, I'll model it exclusively for you,' she murmured.

There was a pregnant pause. 'I'm sorry, *cara,* I have a late meeting scheduled. Can you be ready to leave for the party at seven-thirty?'

'Con...' Discovering that he had cut the call, she dropped her phone into her bag and started walking back to the apartment. Her brow wrinkled. Something was going on that she did not understand. The few times that they'd had sex it had been amazing for both of them. Constantin could not have faked his groans of pleasure as he'd come inside her.

Nor was it conceivable that he had become bored of her already. He was always up and dressed when she woke in the mornings, but she'd seen the way he looked at her with a feral gleam in his eyes and she knew he wanted to join her back in bed. So why didn't he? Was he under pressure at work, or was something else bothering him?

She sighed as she let herself into the penthouse. Maybe, like her, he was wondering where their relationship was going. By silent, mutual agreement they hadn't discussed the state of their marriage, but Constantin had not refuted reports in the Italian media that they were reconciled, and there had been several photos of them together in the newspapers.

He arrived home at ten past seven and walked into the bedroom to find her in her underwear as she was getting changed for the party. To Isobel's astonishment dull colour flared on his cheekbones as he studied her black lace thong and matching push-up bra, before he muttered something incomprehensible and shot into the bathroom like a one-hundred-metre sprinter.

Enough was enough, Isobel decided. When her virile, stallion of a husband started acting like a shy virgin, it was time to demand some answers.

Constantin stiffened when he felt two slender arms wrap around his waist. Isobel had stepped behind him in the shower cubicle but the noise of the spray had muffled her arrival, and now he was in trouble. Stiff was an apt description of a certain part of his anatomy, he thought derisively. He did not need to glance down to know that he was massively aroused, and her throaty murmur of approval made a bad situation even worse.

All week, he had tried to keep his distance from her. His nightmare had scared the hell out of him. Isobel was the only woman who stirred blood-boiling jealousy in his gut. Look how he had reacted to the waiter! The guy had only smiled at her but Constantin had wanted to rip his head off.

He did not want to feel the possessive, manic jealousy that had gripped his father. He did not want to *feel* any emotions. Somehow he had to get whatever it was he felt for Isobel under control, but every time he made love to her he felt himself slipping deeper beneath her sensual spell. The solution, he'd concluded, was to resist the temptation of her gorgeous body. But her hands were creating havoc and ruining his good intentions.

He couldn't restrain a groan as she skimmed her fingers over his stomach and thighs and along the length of his arousal. 'Isa…bella,' he said through gritted teeth, 'we don't have time before the party.' He made a last-ditch attempt to stop her roving hands.

She slipped round in front of him and kissed his lips. 'It doesn't start until eight o'clock. You must have misread the invitation.' She wrapped her fingers around him and gave him a smile of pure witchery. 'Anyway I have a feeling this won't take long.'

Constantin sucked in a harsh breath as she dropped to her knees and replaced her hands with her mouth. *Madonna*, how could he fight his gut-aching desire for her when she was running her tongue lightly over the sensitive tip? It was all he could do not to spill his seed into her mouth. Only a man with ice running through his veins could resist his beautiful, generous, *bold* Isobel. But Constantin's blood was on fire. Giving a muffled curse, he lifted her into his arms and as she hooked her legs around his waist he entered her with a deep thrust that drove them both close to the edge.

It was urgent and intense, and it couldn't last. After a week of sexual frustration, the excitement of their primitive coupling was electrifying. Isobel dug her fingernails into Constantin's bunched shoulders, anchoring herself to him as he cupped her bottom and pumped into her with hard, fast strokes until she sobbed his name over and over. Her man, her master, she belonged to him and he claimed her utterly, bringing her to a shattering orgasm that sent shudders of indescribable pleasure through her body. His climax was no less spectacular, and at the exquisite moment of release he threw his head back and let out a savage groan before burying his face against her throat while their hearts thundered in unison.

Afterwards Isobel had to rush to get ready for the party. Luckily she had gained a light golden tan from a week in the Italian sunshine and needed nothing more than a coat of mascara to define her eyelashes and a slick of rose-coloured gloss on her lips.

'You look stunning,' Constantin commented quietly when she joined him in the lounge. She had already taken his breath away once this evening, but the sight of her in the floor-length scarlet silk gown held in place with narrow diamanté shoulder straps evoked a curious tightness in his chest.

'It's a beautiful dress.' She did a little twirl in front of the mirror and threw him an impish smile. 'I have a present for you.'

He gave her an intent look as she handed him a black leather box with the distinctive DSE logo embossed on the lid. The platinum wrist watch nestled on a velvet cushion was the most prestigious and expensive watch in the DSE range, and it happened to be his personal favourite.

'You told me that your watch had developed a fault and needed to be repaired. I thought you might like this one to replace the old one.'

'I don't know what to say.' Constantin was aware of a curious scratchiness in his throat. He knew exactly how much the watch was worth in financial terms, but even more touching was the fact that Isobel had chosen this particular model from the collection for him. He smiled. 'This is the first present I've been given since I was eight years old.'

'Apart from Christmas and birthday presents, I suppose you mean.'

'My father didn't believe in celebrating holidays or

personal milestones after my mother died.' His voice became reflective. '*Madre* gave me a model of a sports car for my eighth birthday. Her cancer was untreatable by then and she died a few weeks later.'

Isobel was struck by the lack of emotion in his voice. She was reminded of when she'd had the miscarriage and he had been so matter-of-fact. 'It must have been a terribly sad time for you and your father when your mother died,' she said softly.

For a fleeting moment an indefinable expression crossed his face, but he shrugged and said levelly, 'Life goes on.' He slid the watch onto his wrist. 'Thank you. This is the best present I've ever received.'

Considering that the only other present Constantin had been given was a toy car when he was eight, his enthusiasm for the watch she had bought him was not surprising, Isobel mused later that evening.

She glanced around the packed ballroom of the five-star hotel that had been refurbished by the fabulously wealthy Bonucci family. The décor was opulent and unashamedly luxurious and the guests at the opening party included many of the social elite not just from Rome but across Europe. It was the sort of event that she had dreaded when she had first married Constantin. She had felt awkward and out of place among his sophisticated friends and had convinced herself that they regarded her as a cheap gold-digger.

Despite the fact that she now had a successful career and had 'made it' some of those old, insecure feelings returned as Constantin escorted her around the ballroom and introduced her to the other guests. Their exquisite manners when they greeted her did not disguise the speculative glances they gave her as Constantin slipped his arm around her waist. Isobel told herself she was imagining the coolness she sensed from one or two of the guests, but when Constantin murmured in her ear that he had spotted a business associate he wanted to speak to, she had to fight the temptation to cling to his arm as she had done in the past.

She reminded herself that she had attended countless parties and functions in the past two years and could hold her own in any social situation. She did not need Constantin as a prop. But the sight of a familiar figure making a beeline for her across the ballroom made her heart sink.

'Isobel! I must admit that I did not expect to see *you* here tonight.' Ghislaine Montenocci had recently married, and pictures of her fabulous wedding to a French duke had filled the pages of a well-known celebrity magazine. 'My husband, Duc Alphonse de Cavarre, is over there,' she lost no time in telling Isobel, waving her hand towards a sandy-haired man who looked a good twenty years older than his new wife. Isobel wondered if the social-climbing Ghislaine had been attracted to her husband's title.

'I heard rumours that you and Constantin had reconciled, but I didn't believe it. You must be *so* relieved that he has taken you back.'

Ghislaine's name had changed with her marriage, but unfortunately her personality hadn't, Isobel mused, recalling the other woman's nasty comment that when she had married Constantin she had secured a meal ticket for life.

The insecure Isobel of three years ago had been overawed by Ghislaine, but now she smiled coolly. 'Why relieved?' she queried.

'Well, I would have thought that, having managed to marry a billionaire, you wouldn't want to lose him,' Ghislaine said cattily.

'As a matter of fact, Constantin supported my decision to establish my singing career during the past two years.' It was laughably far from the truth, but Isobel refused to be beaten by Ghislaine. 'I think it is so important for women to have aspirations and a *purpose* in life, rather than simply being a wife, don't you agree?' Isobel guessed that Ghislaine had never done a day's work in her life, and, although it was not in her nature to be unkind, she could not help feeling a little sense of victory when the other woman flushed. 'A strong marriage is one where both partners are able to fulfil their dreams. I admit that I am proud of my career success.'

'So you should be.' Constantin's deep voice behind her made Isobel jump, and her heart did that annoying leap that it always did when he slid his arm around her waist and gave her a sexy smile before he spoke to Ghislaine.

'Isobel and her band the Stone Ladies are amazing, aren't they? I am incredibly proud of my talented wife.'

Ghislaine muttered something about needing to join her husband and moved away. Isobel frowned at Constantin. 'There was no need for you to pretend that you are proud of me. I can fight my own battles,' she said drily.

Something in his bright blue eyes caused her breath to become trapped in her throat.

'I wasn't pretending. I *am* proud of you, Isabella. You weren't born into wealth and privilege like I was, or like Ghislaine. Everything you have achieved has been through your talent, hard work and determination.'

Isobel swallowed the lump that had formed in her throat. 'But you resented the time I spent performing with the band. You blamed my career for driving us apart.'

Constantin grimaced. 'I didn't understand how important music and singing were to you. I believed you preferred to spend time with your friends than with me, and deep down I knew I could not blame you,' he admitted roughly. He met her gaze, and Isobel saw regret in his eyes. 'I had my reasons for drawing away from you, and I see now that you thought I was rejecting you.' He glanced around the crowded ballroom. 'This is not the place to discuss our relationship, *cara,*' he said ruefully. 'I'll go and get us a drink.'

Isobel watched him stride across the room to the bar and had the strangest feeling that he felt tense at the prospect of a discussion about their relationship that was long overdue. She had been stunned to hear him say he was proud of her career. His admiration meant a lot, she acknowledged. For so long she had lived in the shadow of her clever brother, and her failure to match Simon's academic achievements or fulfil her father's expectations had made her feel useless and unworthy of the rich, handsome, successful man she had married. Now she felt she was Constantin's equal, but was it too late for them to turn their marriage around and be lifelong partners?

She studied him as he stopped on his way to the bar to chat to someone. They had lost their child, and he was under no obligation to remain married to her, so why had he told her that he had changed his mind and wanted to give their marriage another chance, unless—her heart thudded against her ribs—could it be that he felt something for her?

'Your husband is a handsome devil. I remember he was a good-looking boy, but then it's hardly surprising when his mother was one of the most photographed models of her era.'

Isobel turned towards the woman who had come to stand next to her. She had met Diane Rivolli when Constantin had introduced them at a dinner party two nights ago, and she remembered he had said that Diane lived outside Rome, near to Casa Celeste on the shores of Lake Albano.

'Did you know Constantin's mother?'

'I knew Susie when she was Susie Hoffman. We belonged to the same modelling agency in New York but Susie was gorgeous and she got far more bookings than any of the other girls.' Diane shrugged. 'In fact I met my husband when Susie invited me to stay at Casa Celeste after she'd married Franco De Severino. I think she was lonely, shut away in that huge house that's more like a museum than a home. As for her husband...'

Diane paused, and Isobel's curiosity grew. 'What about Constantin's father?'

'Franco was a cold fish. I gained the impression that the only thing he cared about was Susie. But he loved her *too* much, if that makes sense?' Seeing Isobel's puzzled expression, Diane tried to explain. 'Franco was obsessed with Susie. He disliked her having friends, and although my husband and I only lived a short distance away we were hardly ever invited to Casa Celeste. On the few occasions when we were invited, Franco was always on edge. He hated other men looking at his wife. I even think he was jealous of his own son,' Diane said meditatively. 'Susie doted on Constantin, but even when he was a baby Franco seemed to resent her spending time with her son. I caught him looking at Constantin once with such a strange expression on his face, as if he hated the child.'

Isobel was fascinated to hear about Constantin's family. She had often wondered why he was reluctant to talk about his childhood. 'Franco must have been devastated when Susie died.'

'You would think so, but if he was upset he didn't show it. At her funeral he stood in the church like a cold statue without a flicker of emotion on his face.' Diane shook her head. 'I found it even stranger that Constantin never cried for his mother. He stood stiffly at Susie's graveside like a miniature image of his father and didn't shed a tear. I didn't see him again for years because Franco packed him off to boarding school. Constantin must have been about sixteen when Franco married his second wife.'

'I had no idea that Constantin had a stepmother.' Isobel frowned at this new revelation. 'He's never mentioned her.'

'Maybe that's because he was in love with Lorena.' Diane paused again, allowing her startling suggestion to register with Isobel.

'Constantin was in love with his stepmother?'

The other woman shrugged. 'Why not? Lorena was much younger than Franco. She was probably only in her early twenties, very attractive—and she knew it! It was pretty obvious that she had married Franco for his money. She enjoyed socialising and she often invited me and my husband to pool parties, although it was clear that Franco hated having visitors.

'I suppose you couldn't blame Lorena for wanting to have fun with Constantin when she was stuck with a dour older husband. She turned the boy's head, flirting with him and paying him attention.' Diane frowned. 'There was something quite cruel about the way Lorena deliberately encouraged Constantin's crush on her, and the way she played father and son off against each other. Franco was jealous of his second wife in the same way he had been with Susie. He was furious if another man so much as looked at her, and Constantin's puppy-dog devotion to Lorena created a lot of friction between father and son.

'I don't know what would have happened if the situation had continued,' Diane went on, 'but then Franco and Lorena died in that terrible accident. Poor Constantin, not only did he witness what happened, but the leadership of DSE was thrown into chaos.

'Constantin should have automatically become joint Chairman and CEO when his father died, but, because he wasn't eighteen, his father's brother, Alonso, assumed control of the company. Constantin worked his way up to CEO, and it's no secret that he wants complete control of DSE.'

Diane took a sip of champagne before continuing. 'It's my belief that Constantin would go to any lengths to claim the chairmanship of DSE that he thinks is his birthright.'

Isobel's head was reeling from everything Diane had said, and she only vaguely registered the bit about Constantin wanting to be Chairman of DSE. Why hadn't he told her that his father and stepmother had died in an accident when he had been a young man? The tragedy must have had a fundamental impact on Constantin, especially if he had been in love with Lorena. Could it explain his strange behaviour when he had taken her to Casa Celeste? she wondered. Had he become cold and remote with her because he was *still* in love with his stepmother?

'What actually happened to Constantin's father and stepmother?'

Diane gave her a strange look. 'You mean he hasn't told you?' She seemed suddenly flustered when she caught sight of him walking across the ballroom towards them. 'I've probably said too much. Why don't you ask Constantin what took place at the top of the tower at Casa Celeste?'

CHAPTER TEN

'THE HOUSE IS shut up and unstaffed apart from a caretaker and gardener because I rarely go there. I don't understand why you want to visit Casa Celeste.'

'I've told you why. I want to visit Arianna's grave.' Isobel held Constantin's gaze and refused to be intimidated by the impatient expression etched on his taut features. 'I don't need staff. I'm perfectly capable of making up a bed and cooking meals.'

He frowned at her across the breakfast bar where they had been enjoying a leisurely Saturday morning breakfast until she had stated her wish to make the twenty-kilometre journey south of the city to Lake Albano. 'I don't see the point…'

'Your lack of understanding says a lot,' she interrupted him, struggling to hide the hurt in her voice. 'You've obviously been able to forget about our daughter, but I haven't, nor do I want to forget her. I would like to spend some time at the chapel where she's buried.'

Last night, when they had arrived home from the party, she had tried to talk about the past and in particular the things Diane Rivolli had said about Constantin's father and stepmother being involved in a terrible accident at Casa Celeste. But Constantin had refused to be drawn into a discussion, and had distracted her by sweeping her into his arms and whispering in her ear exactly what he was going to do to her once he had removed her dress and the tantalising wisps of her black lace underwear that he had pictured in his mind all evening.

Resistance would be futile, he had warned her. But Isobel had had no intention of resisting him, and by the time he had kissed her senseless before trailing his lips down her body to bestow a wickedly intimate caress that had resulted in her shuddering orgasm, she had forgotten that she had wanted to talk to him. When they had made love last night she had felt closer to him than she had ever felt, and, waking in his arms this morning, she had been filled with optimism that they had a future together. But her request to visit Casa Celeste had created a distinct chill in the atmosphere.

'It's never a good idea to revisit the past,' he said harshly.

'That's your way of dealing with things, isn't it? You pretend they never happened and refuse to talk about them. Are you going to keep running away for ever, Constantin?' Isobel said bitterly. She looked away from him. 'I've come to terms with the miscarriage, but our baby will always have a special place in my heart. I'm going to Casa Celeste, with or without you.'

Constantin's jaw clenched. He did not know how to handle this confident Isobel who wasn't afraid to argue with him. She had changed immeasurably in the two years they had been apart, although her sensuality and generosity when they made love still set her apart from any of his previous lovers, he brooded, feeling his body stir as he remembered the erotic session in the shower that had made them late for the Bonuccis' party.

'I can't spend time away from the office right now,' he said curtly. 'I don't want you to go to the house on your own while the stalker is still a threat to your safety. For all we know, he could have discovered that you are in Rome.'

'The police in England have arrested David and he is receiving psychiatric care. They phoned with the news yesterday and I meant to tell you when you came home from work, but...' she blushed as X-rated images of them in the shower flooded her mind '...we were distracted.'

'Hmm...*distracted* is one way to describe what we were doing,' Constantin murmured. He walked round the breakfast bar and lifted her off the bar stool, holding her so that her pelvis was in burning contact with his. 'Why don't we go back to bed and distract each other some more, *mia bella*?'

It was hard to think straight when his lips were trailing a sensual path along her collarbone. Isobel felt a familiar melting sensation in the pit of her stomach as he began to unbutton her shirt. She definitely should have worn a bra, she mused, stifling a moan when he rubbed his thumb pads across her nipples and they instantly hardened. All week, when he had rushed off to work each morning, she had longed for him to stay home and make slow leisurely love to her, but now she fought the temptation of his roaming hands and mouth. She recognised his diversionary tactics and refused to be sidetracked from her determination to go to Casa Celeste.

She had told him the truth when she'd said she wanted to visit their baby's grave. But she also sensed that there were secrets at the De Severino's ancestral home that she needed to uncover if she was to have a chance of understanding her enigmatic husband.

'I know what game you're playing, Constantin,' she told him. She slid out of his arms and refastened her shirt, wincing as the cotton brushed across the sensitive peaks of her breasts. 'It won't work. Either you come with me to Casa Celeste, or I'll go there on my own before I catch the next flight back to England.'

Constantin gave her a frustrated look. 'That sounds like blackmail.' He remembered making the same accusation to his uncle not so long ago.

The stubborn set of Isobel's jaw infuriated him. She used to be so amenable! 'I'm tempted to put you over my knee,' he growled, and had the satisfaction of seeing her eyes widen and her cheeks suffuse with colour. 'But if I did, I guarantee we wouldn't leave the bedroom for a week.'

Constantin suddenly decided that he had to make several urgent business calls, and he spent all afternoon in his study, meaning that they did not set out for Casa Celeste until early evening. He was uncommunicative during the journey to Lake Albano, and when the car turned through the gates of the De Severino estate onto a long driveway lined with poplar trees he tightened his hands on the steering wheel so that his knuckles whitened.

Diane Rivolli's suggestion that Isobel should ask him about the accident that had resulted in the deaths of his father and stepmother was not as simple as it seemed, she brooded as she glanced at him. His grim expression did not encourage her to probe into his past, but she was convinced that they could not have a future together unless she could find the key that would unlock his emotions.

Her thoughts were diverted as they drew up in front of the house. The first time Isobel had visited Casa Celeste she had been awed by the grandeur of the four-storey building with its tall windows, elegant columns, and a tall tower topped with a spire that gave the house the look of a fairy-tale castle. Inside was no less magnificent. The frescoes on the walls and ceilings were adorned with gold leaf, and the white marble floors created an ambiance of welcome coolness to visitors entering the house from the heat of the Italian sun.

Diane had been right when she'd said that Casa Celeste was more like a museum than a home, Isobel acknowledged as she walked past a row of portraits of Constantin's ancestors. It was something she had thought herself when she had stayed there in the past. The dust sheets draped over the furniture added to the impression that this was a house of ghosts.

She shivered. It had been in this house that she had suffered a miscarriage. Shortly after dinner one evening she had been violently sick. The doctor Constantin called out had initially thought she had food poisoning, but the stomach cramps had worsened, and when she had started to bleed she had been rushed into hospital, but nothing could be done to save the baby.

It's never a good idea to revisit the past, Constantin had warned her before they had left Rome. She wondered what memories filled his mind when he came to Casa Celeste. Blinking back her tears, she walked outside to the courtyard at the back of the house and found him sitting on a low wall surrounding an ornamental fountain.

'Why didn't you tell me that your father and his second wife died here at Casa Celeste?'

He stiffened and shot her a searching look. 'I suppose Diane was gossiping,' he said tersely. 'No doubt she filled your head with lurid tales.'

'Diane didn't tell me anything, except that they had been killed in an accident which you witnessed.' The cold gleam in Constantin's eyes warned Isobel that he wanted her to drop the subject, but her determination to resolve the issues that she was sure had come between them during their marriage made her press him for an answer. 'What actually happened?'

A nerve flickered in his jaw. 'Are you sure you want to know? Be careful, Isobel. Some secrets are best left hidden.'

She did not know how to respond, and after a few moments he shrugged and glanced up at the tall tower attached to the main house. His voice was devoid of emotion when he spoke.

'My father and stepmother fell to their deaths from the balcony up there at the top of the tower.' He kicked the hard cobblestoned courtyard. 'They were both killed instantly, which was some small mercy, I suppose.'

She gave a horrified gasp. 'You saw it happen?'

'Yes. It wasn't pretty, as I'm sure you can imagine.' His tone was so matter-of-fact that he could have been discussing something as mundane as the weather.

Isobel was lost for words, shocked not just by the details of the fatal accident but by Constantin's lack of sentiment. 'What a terrible thing to have witnessed. You must have had nightmares afterwards...' Her voice faltered as she remembered how she had heard him shouting out during the night when they had stayed at Casa Celeste. No wonder his cries had been so blood-curdling if his dreams had relived the horror of seeing his father and stepmother plunge to their deaths.

'You should have told me.' She felt hurt that he had not confided in her about the traumatic event in his life that must have affected him—and quite possibly *still* affected him, she mused, remembering what she had heard about Constantin's relationship with his father's second wife. 'At least I would have understood why you dislike coming here.' She bit her lip. 'Diane said that you were in love with Lorena.'

His reaction was explosive. He jumped to his feet and slashed his hand through the air. '*Mio Dio!* That woman should have her tongue cut out. Diane Rivolli was never party to my thoughts. She knows *nothing*, and she has no right to make slanderous accusations about me.'

He had paled beneath his tan, and the hand he raked through his hair shook, Isobel noticed. It was the first time she had ever seen him so worked up. Gone was his air of cool detachment. His jaw was rigid and his eyes glittered with anger. 'I warned you that the past is best left dead and buried,' he said savagely.

'Constantin…' She stared after him as he strode out of a gate in the courtyard wall that led to dense woodland surrounding the house, which was home to wild boar. He had once told her that *cinghiale* could weigh up to four hundred pounds and the males had fearsome tusks. But a wild boar was probably not as dangerous as Constantin's mood was right now, Isobel thought ruefully. His violent reaction when she had mentioned his father's young wife pointed to him having been in love with Lorena.

She suddenly wished she had heeded his advice and stayed away from Casa Celeste. There was a strange atmosphere in the courtyard where Franco and Lorena had died. The sun sinking below the horizon was blood-red, and cast long shadows on the house. Despite the warm evening air Isobel shivered as goosebumps prickled her skin, and, giving a low cry, she ran back inside. But there was no comfort to be found in the coldly elegant rooms. Casa Celeste was an impressive house, but she wondered if it had ever felt like a home to Constantin.

She unloaded the car and carried the food they had brought with them into the kitchen, where she put together a salad, forced herself to eat a small dinner, and put the rest in the fridge for Constantin, if and when he returned

later. He still had not come back when she made up the bed
in the master bedroom, before choosing one of the guest
bedrooms for herself. She avoided the bedroom where she
had stayed on her last disastrous visit two years ago.

Constantin's revelation about the tragedy that he had
witnessed at Casa Celeste went some way to explaining
why he disliked the house, but there were so many things
about him that she still did not understand. Her marriage
was as full of secrets as it had always been and she was
no closer to discovering what, if anything, Constantin felt
for her.

She must have slept deeply, because she did not hear
him enter her bedroom much later that night, and she was
unaware that he stood by the bed for a long time, a grave,
almost tortured expression on his face as he watched her
sleeping.

When Isobel opened her eyes, bright sunlight filled the
room and she immediately saw Constantin sitting in an
armchair next to the window.

'You look terrible,' she told him bluntly, raking her eyes
over his haggard face and the black stubble covering his
jaw. 'Have you slept at all?'

Instead of answering her question, he said harshly,
'Let's go back to Rome. There is evil here in this house.'

She nodded slowly. 'I can understand why you think
that. But our daughter is here. I'm not leaving until I've
visited Arianna's grave.'

The tiny private chapel where for centuries the members of
the De Severino family had been baptised and buried was
a little way off from the house. Isobel followed a path that
wound through the estate, passing olive groves and vine-
yards before she caught sight of the ancient stone building. When she had last been there, on the day of Arianna's

funeral, the chapel grounds had been overgrown and sunlight had struggled to filter through the trees. She remembered how she had felt hollow with grief and utterly alone. Constantin had been with her, but she had been chilled by his lack of emotion as they had said goodbye to their baby.

The gloomy surroundings had augmented her misery on that day two and a half years ago. But as she pushed open the gate and walked towards Arianna's headstone she was shocked to see that dozens of rose bushes had been planted around the grave, and a bench had been placed nearby beneath the delicate fronds of a young weeping willow. The tall oak trees had been cut back allowing sunshine to bathe this corner of the graveyard in a golden halo of light.

Isobel stopped in her tracks and stared. She caught sight of an elderly gardener pruning a hedge and walked over to him.

'The roses are beautiful. It must have taken a lot of work to plant so many.'

His lined face creased into a smile. 'Not for me. *Il Marchese* planted them for his *bambina*. He comes often. Not to the house. He sits there.' The old man nodded to the bench. 'There is peace here.'

Isobel understood. The only sound was birdsong and the whisper of the breeze gently stirring the willow tree. The gardener moved away, leaving her alone to admire the roses that were just coming into bloom. All the bushes had pink buds, she realised. Pink for a girl. In the hushed stillness of the garden she thought she heard tinkling laughter. Her vision was blurred with tears and for a moment she was sure she glimpsed a little figure running along the path.

'Arianna!'

She whirled round, but no one was there. The ache in

her throat became unbearable and she sank down onto the bench and allowed her tears to fall.

'I knew it was a mistake to come.' Constantin's voice, deep as an ocean, sounded close by. Isobel had been unaware that he had followed her from the house. 'I knew you would find it too painful,' he said thickly. He sat down on the bench and pulled her into his arms, but said nothing more, simply held her and stroked her hair while she wept.

At last she lifted her head and scrubbed her wet face with the back of her hand. 'I'm not only crying for Arianna. I'm sad because I didn't know how much losing her hurt you.'

She waved her hand at the rose garden. 'You created this beautiful place in memory of our baby, but I had no idea that you cared. You were so distant, so…contained and unemotional. I needed you,' she told him in a choked voice. 'I wish we could have grieved together. I was angry because I believed you didn't feel the pain I felt. I even thought that you hadn't wanted our baby. Why couldn't you have told me that you were sad too?'

'I couldn't,' he said heavily. 'I can't explain.'

'Please try, because I want to understand,' she whispered.

Something flared in his eyes, but he turned his head away from her tear-streaked face and said nothing.

'Diane said that you didn't cry at your mother's funeral. I don't understand. You were eight years old and I know you loved her. You keep the model sports car she gave you for your birthday locked in a glass cabinet.'

'My father told me I mustn't cry,' Constantin said harshly. 'He said that crying was a sign of weakness and De Severino men are not weak.'

'So that's why your father didn't show any emotion

when he stood at your mother's grave. Diane said…' Her
voice faltered when he frowned.

'Diane obviously said a damn sight too much.'

His mouth twisted. As Constantin had walked through
the grounds of the chapel and heard Isobel weeping he'd
felt a pain beneath his breastbone, as if his heart had splin-
tered. His first instinct had been to leave her to grieve
alone as he had done when she'd had the miscarriage. But
something had made him turn back to her. *Are you going
to keep running away for ever?* she had asked him.

Dio! She had made him take a long, hard look at himself, and he had felt ashamed. Since he was a boy, he had
believed that emotions were a sign of weakness. But who
was the coward—brave, strong Isobel who was honest
about her feelings? Or him, a grown man too scared to
allow himself to feel the emotional highs and lows that
were part of life?

'Diane did not see what I saw.'

Isobel stared at him, shocked by the rawness in his
voice. 'What did you see?'

He shook his head and hunched forwards, his shoulders
bowed. 'I saw my father crying.'

Constantin was eight years old again, standing outside
his father's study listening to the terrible moans coming
from behind the closed door. He'd been scared that a *cinghiale* had got into the house and was goring his father with
its sharp tusks. His heart had thudded beneath his ribs as
he'd slowly pushed open the door.

'On the night my mother was buried I heard strange
noises from my father's study,' he told Isobel. 'I went in
and saw him rolling on the floor as though he was in
agony.' Constantin let out a ragged breath. 'Franco was
crying in a way I'd never seen anyone cry before. I was
just a child…and I was frightened. My father had told me

that only weak men cried. He looked up and saw me and he was angry, shouting at me to go away. I ran to the door, but he called to me. "Now you know how cruel love is, how it brings a man to utter despair and misery."'

Constantin could hear his father's voice. He glanced at Isobel and saw a mixture of shock and sympathy in her hazel eyes that tugged on something deep inside him.

'The next day, my father was his usual, cold self. Neither of us ever spoke about what had happened, but I sensed he was ashamed that I had witnessed his breakdown. He sent me away to school and I saw very little of him when I was growing up. But the memory of him sobbing, and the realisation that love had reduced my proud father to a broken man, stayed in my mind. I was frightened by the destructive power of love, and how it could make a man weak. At eight years old I learned to keep my emotions locked inside me.'

'But you did care about our baby,' Isobel said softly. 'You couldn't cry for Arianna, but you planted this garden for her.'

She stood up and walked among the rose bushes, leaning down to inhale the delicate perfume of the unfurling petals. Her heart ached. She felt unbearably moved by Constantin's admission that he could not show his emotions, but Arianna's garden was proof that he had shared her devastation at the loss of their daughter.

Constantin broke off a rosebud from a bush and handed it to her before he swept her up in his arms.

'What are you doing?' Her breath left her body in a shaky sigh. The temptation to rest her aching head on his shoulder was too strong to resist.

'What I should have done two years ago. I'm going to take care of you, *tesorino*,' he said softly. 'I'm going to run you a bath, and I'm going to cook dinner for you—'

he looked into her eyes, and Isobel's heart leapt at the sensual promise in his gaze '—and then I am going to make love to you.'

'You can't carry me all the way back to the house,' she murmured. But he did, and when he entered the cool marble hallway of Casa Celeste he continued up the stairs to the master bedroom and into the en suite bathroom, where he filled the sunken bath with water and added a handful of rose-scented crystals.

His hands were gentle as he unbuttoned her shirt and placed it on the chair before he removed her skirt and underwear. She gathered her hair up and pinned it on top of her head, exposing her slender neck.

'You're beautiful,' he said roughly. 'I knew the moment I saw you that I was in trouble.' He turned to walk out of the bathroom, but she touched his arm.

'After I lost the baby I felt angry when you suggested we make love because I thought it was proof that you didn't care.'

He shook his head. 'I didn't know how else to reach out to you. Bed was the one place where we understood each other's needs perfectly, and I wanted to show you what I couldn't say with words. I knew I had failed you. I knew you wanted more support from me...' his voice became husky '...but the truth is that hearing you crying was something I couldn't deal with. When you pushed me away, I told myself it was no more than I deserved. I decided to wait until you gave some sign that you wanted me.'

Isobel glanced ruefully at her swollen nipples. Her breasts felt heavy and the sweet ache between her legs could only be assuaged by Constantin. 'In case you've missed the signs my body is sending you, I want you,' she said softly.

His chest lifted as he drew a jerky breath. She looked

heartbreakingly fragile and emotionally spent. 'You need food, rest...'

She stepped towards him and reached up to brush her mouth lightly across his. 'I need you.'

Luckily it was a big bath. He helped her step into the water and slid in behind her. She leaned back against his chest and sank deep into a world of pleasure, where nothing existed but the drift of his hands on her body as he caressed her breasts, cupping them and feeling their weight, before he moved lower.

'Mind where you put that bar of soap,' she murmured and heard his husky chuckle in her ear as he dropped the soap and used his fingers in an intimate exploration that made her catch her breath. 'Constantin...' Her voice was urgent as she felt her pleasure build. Liquid heat pooled between her thighs and she tried to turn towards him.

'This is for you, *tesorino*.' He held her firmly in place and used his fingers to wicked effect while his other hand stole up to her breasts to tease each rose-tipped point in turn until her breathing quickened. He felt the sudden tension in her muscles, and he held her there, poised on the brink for a few seconds before sliding his fingers deeply into her to capture the frantic pulse of her orgasm.

Afterwards he dried her with a soft towel and smoothed fragrant oil over every centimetre of her skin, paying such careful attention to certain areas of her body that Isobel ached to take him inside her. Somehow they made it into the bedroom, and he placed her on the edge of the bed and stood between her legs, spreading her wide and sliding his hands beneath her bottom to angle her for his complete possession.

Their eyes met, held, and time stood still. There was no teasing gleam in his bright blue gaze now, just a stark need that touched Isobel's heart and made her think of the young boy who had stood beside his mother's grave and forced his lips not to tremble and his tears not to fall.

There were still many unanswered questions, but he had been right when he'd said that when they made love they understood each other perfectly.

There was no need for words. Their bodies moved in total accord and she arched beneath him to meet each powerful thrust as he drove her higher and higher. She sensed he was holding back, and his infinite care brought tears to her eyes. Tenderness was a new element to his desire and she loved him all the more for it, but what she needed right now was his hunger, his primitive need to claim her as his own.

There was no need for words. She told him in her evocative kiss that shook him with its innate sensuality exactly what she wanted from him. Passion, raw and honest and demanding a response she gave him with a willingness that rocked him to the depths of his soul as they climaxed simultaneously and tumbled together in a glorious freefall.

A long time later, hunger of a different kind prompted Constantin to head downstairs to the kitchen to prepare the dinner he had promised Isobel. They had picked up steaks and salad on the drive to the house, and the cellar offered a wide selection of vintage wines. He chose a fifteen-year-old Barolo, collected glasses and cutlery and set a table outside on the terrace overlooking an informal flower garden.

The mingled scents of jasmine and night-scented stocks greeted Isobel as she sat down opposite Constantin. Her heart fluttered madly like a trapped bird beneath her ribcage as she stared at the jewellery case he placed in front of her. The yellow diamond solitaire he had given her when he had asked her to marry him, the day after she had told him she was expecting his baby, lay next to the plain gold wedding band she had pulled from her finger before she had rushed out of the house in Grosvenor Square two years ago.

She lifted her eyes to his, silently questioning him.

'I would like you to wear your rings again, Isabella,' he said levelly.

He did not embellish the statement with flowery phrases, or say that he loved her, but she had not expected him to. Maybe he would never be able to share his feelings in words, but hadn't he shown her when he had made love to her with tender passion that he believed they shared something special?

But was it enough? She bit her lip. 'My career…?'

'Will, I'm confident, continue to go from strength to strength. I listened to the Stone Ladies' latest album while I was making dinner, and there is no doubt that all the members of the band are talented musicians, but you especially, *cara*. You have an exceptional voice.'

He was blown away by her talent, Constantin thought to himself. Isobel had a gift for singing and song writing, but when they had been together he'd been jealous of the time she spent with the other band members and he had not been supportive or understood why having a career was so important to her.

He picked up her wedding ring and felt her hand tremble as he slid the gold band onto her third finger. Her diamond engagement ring caught a moonbeam and sparkled with fiery brilliance that reflected the fire in her eyes.

'Food,' he said huskily, uncovering the serving plates where he had piled the grilled steaks. 'Something tells me I'm going to need plenty of protein for strength and stamina tonight.'

'Believe it,' she told him sweetly. 'You have two years to make up for.'

The sultry gleam in his eyes heightened Isobel's anticipation, as did his murmured, 'I will endeavour to give you complete satisfaction, *tesorino*.'

CHAPTER ELEVEN

THE SEQUENCE OF events was familiar. The sound of raised voices at the top of the tower. He looked up and saw his father and stepmother. Lorena was falling, screaming— and then her screams stopped. There was so much blood. It was on his hands as he knelt beside her, rolled her over and saw that it wasn't Lorena, but Isobel, lying lifeless on the ground. And now he was standing on the balcony at the top of the tower, stretching his hands towards Isobel. There was blood on his hands.

No! *Mio Dio*, no!

Constantin jerked upright, panting, his breath coming in short, sharp bursts like a marathon runner pushing himself towards the finishing post. He ran a trembling hand across his brow and turned his head slowly, almost scared of what he might see on the pillow beside him. The pale gold of dawn's first light drifted through the half-open curtains and played in Isobel's hair. Her face, flushed rose-pink in sleep, was serene and so lovely that his stomach muscles clenched. There was no blood, and she wasn't lying in a crumpled heap at the base of the tower. He had been dreaming.

Taking care not to wake her, he slid out of bed and walked across to the window. The bedroom overlooked the courtyard. The bloodstains that had covered the cobbles beneath the tower had long since been washed away, but the images in his head, *Dio!* He would never forget what he had witnessed when he had been seventeen, Constantin thought grimly. He would never forget watching his father stretch a hand towards Lorena seconds before she had fallen. His nightmare, like all his other nightmares, was a warning. What if he was truly his father's son? What if he had inherited the monstrous jealousy that had turned Franco into a murderer?

He looked back at Isobel, sleeping peacefully and unaware of the danger she was in. But he knew. He had known from the first night that they had become lovers and he'd had his first nightmare that he should never have got involved with her.

He stood by the window for a long time, lost in his dark thoughts that the sun, rising high in the sky, could not lighten. Isobel stirred but fell back to sleep. Her exhaustion wasn't surprising after they had spent all night pleasuring each other. Constantin closed his eyes and pictured her slender body poised above him as she had lowered herself onto him; her sweet smile as she had taken him deep inside her and their two bodies had become one.

The sound of a car driving into the courtyard below pulled him back to the present. His uncle was early for their meeting. He paused on his way out of the room to look at Isobel. His resolve hardened. The time had come for him to take control of his future.

Isobel stretched languorously and felt a pleasurable ache in certain muscles. Her entire body tingled, especially her breasts and between her legs where Constantin had devoted his lavish attention. Her face grew warm as she recalled vividly the many and varied ways he had made love to her the previous night. She turned her head towards the empty pillow beside her and wished she had woken in his arms. But the clock told her that the morning was nearly afternoon and he had obviously decided that she needed to sleep in after their energetic night.

The diamond on her finger glinted as it caught a sunbeam, and she could not hold back a smile of pure happiness. Last night Constantin had returned her engagement and wedding rings to their rightful place, and today was full of hope and promise for the future.

She heard his voice from the study when she went downstairs, and guessed he was speaking on the phone. Deciding not to disturb him, she continued into the kitchen in search of a caffeine fix. The percolator was bubbling. Her eyes flew to the man seated at the table, sipping a cup of coffee. She recognised him as Constantin's uncle, Alonso, whom she had met briefly when he had been a guest at their wedding.

He stood up as she entered the kitchen and proffered his hand. 'Isobel, I am delighted to find you here at Casa Celeste with your husband.' Alonso spoke in a thick Italian accent.

His words sent a little jolt of surprise through her until she realised that he was looking at her wedding and engagement rings on her finger.

'I'm glad to be here with Constantin,' she murmured as she poured herself a cup of coffee and sat down at the table.

'So, all is well with you and Constantin and you are reconciled. That is good news. The board of DSE are pleased that he has put an end to his playboy image and the newspapers now portray him as a respectable married man. It's amazing what a little coercion can do.'

Isobel set her coffee cup carefully back in its saucer. 'Coercion?' she said faintly. 'I'm not sure I understand.'

'But yes, I prompted my nephew, I…how do you say in English? I gave him a little push to encourage him to resume his marriage.' The elderly man smiled at her. 'I think I do you the favour, hmm? I told Constantin that I would appoint him as Chairman of the company only if he mended his wild ways and returned to his wife.'

'When…' she swallowed, trying to stem the nausea that swept through her '…when did you tell Constantin this?'

He shrugged. 'I know the exact date. It was the fifteenth of this month, my seventieth birthday. I told him that I wanted to retire and I was considering making his cousin Maurio Chairman unless Constantin could convince me that he was ready to commit to DSE by honouring his commitment to his marriage.'

The *sixteenth* of June had been the date of the fund-raising party in London where the Stone Ladies had performed, and later Constantin had kissed her very publicly on the dance floor.

Functioning on autopilot, Isobel drank the rest of her coffee, grimacing as she swallowed the bitter grounds at the bottom of the cup. Constantin had told her that he'd changed his mind and wanted to give their marriage another chance the evening *after* he had been given an ultimatum by his uncle to return to his marriage or lose the chairmanship of DSE.

She had been such a fool! She felt as if the spark of life itself had drained out of her, and her coffee cup slid out of her numb fingers and clattered onto the saucer.

'I can't believe it,' she whispered.

Alonso chuckled, blithely unaware of the bombshell he had dropped. '*Sì*, for me also it is hard to believe I am seventy. I am looking forward to spending more time on the golf course now that Constantin is to be Chairman.'

He looked concerned when he noticed how pale she had gone. 'Are you ill?'

Isobel scraped her chair on the tiled floor as she staggered to her feet. 'I feel a little...*nauseato.*'

'Ah.' Alonso nodded. '*Un bambino,* perhaps?'

Sweet heaven! Her heart missed a beat. Fate would surely not play such a cruel trick as to give her a child now, when she had proof of Constantin's duplicity, she tried to reassure herself as she hurried out of the kitchen. But thudding inside her head was the knowledge that she had left her contraceptive pills behind at her flat in London when Constantin had driven her straight from the hospital to the airport and they had boarded his jet to fly to Rome. When they'd had sex she had completely forgotten that she was not protected.

She was halfway across the hall, marching towards the study, when the door opened and he emerged. '*Tesorino.*' His smiled faded when he saw the grim purpose in her expression.

'Don't *tesorino* me!' she snapped, but her eyes absorbed his male beauty; the sculpted angles of his face, and his powerful body clothed in sun-bleached jeans that clung to his hips and a cream cotton shirt open at the throat to reveal a fuzz of black chest hairs. She would love him until she died and the knowledge fuelled her anger.

'I want the truth.'

He raised an eyebrow, but beneath his nonchalance she sensed that he was as tense and watchful as a jungle cat stalking prey.

'I have never lied to you, Isabella.'

'Did you ask me to give our marriage another chance so that your uncle would appoint you Chairman of DSE instead of your cousin?'

Isobel's question echoed around the marble hall, and

it seemed to Constantin that the air trembled as it waited for him to reply. He watched dust motes dance in a shaft of sunlight streaming through a window, while his mind relived the nightmare he'd had about her. The sun touched Isobel's hair and bathed her in a halo of golden light, and as he stared at her lovely face he suddenly knew what he must do.

He shrugged. '*Mea culpa.* I assume you have spoken to Alonso, so it would be pointless for me to deny it.'

The world rocked beneath Isobel's feet but through sheer force of will she remained standing. She wanted to hurt him as she was hurting, and her hand shot out to connect with his cheek, leaving a scarlet imprint of her fingers on his skin. He flinched, and she felt sick with shame. She abhorred physical violence and she hated herself for her betraying loss of control.

'You bastard,' she choked. 'I suppose you returned my rings last night knowing that Alonso was coming to Casa Celeste today.'

In her mind she heard Diane Rivolli at the Bonuccis' party. *Constantin would go to any lengths to claim the chairmanship of DSE that he thinks is his birthright.*

She tugged her engagement ring and wedding band off her finger and hurled them at him one at a time.

'*You keep them,*' she said hoarsely. Her throat felt as if she had swallowed glass. 'I don't want them. Maybe in the future you'll fool another woman into thinking that you do actually have a heart rather than a lump of stone in your chest, and you can give them to her. But sooner or later she'll discover that there's nothing but an empty, emotionless void where your heart should be.'

The rings bounced off his chest and flew up into the air. The yellow diamond glinted in the sunlight before the two rings fell back to the ground and skidded across the marble floor. Isobel did not see where they landed. She spun away from Constantin and flew across the hall. His car keys were on the table and she snatched them up on her way out of the front door.

'*Isobel!* For Christ's sake be careful,' he shouted after her, sharp urgency in his voice. 'You're not used to driving such a powerful car.'

It was typical that he was more concerned about his car than her, she thought bitterly as she thrust the key into the ignition. The engine roared into life, and when she touched the accelerator pedal the car shot forwards so fast that the tyres spun and sent up sprays of gravel. Tears choked her. Her marriage had been a farce from the start, and now it was over for good.

The sports car was a strong-willed beast that needed to be firmly controlled and as Isobel negotiated the sharp bends along the narrow road leading from Casa Celeste she focused on staying alive. But with every mile that she drove away from Constantin the pain inside her intensified until she could barely breathe and she could no longer hold back her tears.

After a narrow shave with a cart being pulled along the road by a donkey, she turned off into a small village and parked in the central square that was deserted in the middle of the day when the sun was at its hottest and the villagers retreated to their houses.

She cried until her chest hurt. She had been such a fool. When Constantin had told her a few days ago that he had not only married her because she had been pregnant, she had actually believed him. Anger burned in her gut. She wanted to rip his heart out as he had ripped out hers. She wanted him to suffer as she was suffering, but he never would because he was made of stone.

He had deliberately and cold-heartedly used her to gain the chairmanship of DSE. He had seduced her and made love to her, he'd even gone to the length of asking her to wear her wedding ring again—*but it had all been lies*!

She stuffed her fist into her mouth to hold back her cry of pain. She would never, ever forgive him for his cruel deception. Why hadn't she gone ahead with the divorce when he had first asked her, instead of clinging to the stupid hope that he might actually care for her? Memories of her father's lack of interest opened up an old wound. She hadn't been good enough, clever enough—simply not enough for her father, who had loved her brother but not her. It was bitterly ironic that Constantin, the only man she had fallen in love with, had never loved her either.

Wearily, Isobel dug out a tissue from her handbag and wiped her eyes. What had she expected from Constantin? He had told her that he found it difficult to show his emotions, but the truth was that he only cared about one thing and that was DSE. He was driven, ambitious and utterly ruthless.

She took a ragged breath, and was about to turn the ignition key to restart the car when she pictured in her mind the rose garden he had created in memory of their baby. He had chosen pink rosebuds for Arianna, and he had dug the garden himself, laboured long and hard to make a place of beauty and peace where he could sit and remember a little girl who had never lived but had a special place in his heart.

Those were not the actions of a ruthless man, Isobel conceded. She bit her lip, remembering how he had taken care of her after she had been attacked by the stalker. He had been determined to protect her, and had even hired a bodyguard, even though she had told him not to.

But it had been in his interest to protect her, she reminded herself. He had needed to show his uncle that he had reconciled his marriage, and she had just been a pawn in his ambition to take control of DSE…hadn't she?

It was too hot inside the car for her to think straight. She climbed out of the vehicle and locked it. The luxurious sports car was very noticeable in the village square, and a group of small boys were staring at it with wide-eyed fascination. Perhaps all boys loved sports cars, Isobel thought as she walked over to the shade of an oak tree. She remembered the model car that Constantin's mother had given him for his eighth birthday and which he kept locked in a cabinet as if it were as priceless as the crown jewels.

He had loved his mother, but his father had forbidden him to cry at her funeral. Isobel groaned. How could she have expected Constantin to show his emotions when he had been brought up to hide his feelings? He had not cried at Arianna's funeral, but perhaps he cried alone when he sat in the rose garden he had made for her.

She stopped pacing up and down, and hugged her arms around her body, trying to hold her own emotions in check as her treacherous mind recalled his tenderness when he had carried her upstairs to the bedroom last night. His hands had shook as he'd undressed before sweeping her into his arms and kissing her with such beguiling sweetness and breathtaking sensuality that tears had filled her eyes.

Constantin's actions had not been those of a man without a heart, or of a man who did not care.

She would be the biggest fool on the planet if she went back to Casa Celeste, Isobel told herself. The sensible thing to do would be to continue her journey back to Rome and catch the next available flight to London to begin divorce proceedings. Constantin did not deserve another chance. He did not deserve her love.

But she could not dismiss the image in her mind of a little boy standing dry-eyed at his mother's grave. She could not forget the aching sweetness of Constantin's kiss. *She* deserved to know the truth of why he had married her. He owed her that much. Suddenly she was running back to the car, determined to uncover the secrets that she was sure he still hid from her.

CHAPTER TWELVE

THE HOUSE APPEARED to be deserted. Isobel's footsteps echoed hollowly on the marble floor as she walked into the hall. It crossed her mind that Constantin might have asked his uncle for a lift back to Rome, but in that case why was the front door unlocked? There was no sign of him downstairs, and she had just reached the first-floor landing when she heard a noise that froze her blood. The moan of pain had come from the master bedroom. She hurried along the passage and opened the door, and reeled with shock at the sight that met her.

Constantin was sitting on the bed, hunched over, his face buried in his hands, and he was crying—great, tearing sobs that shook his body. Only once before had Isobel seen a man cry so broken-heartedly. Her father had howled like an animal in terrible pain when they had dragged her brother's body from the reservoir. She hadn't known how to comfort her father, and deep down she had wondered if he'd wished that it had been her instead of Simon who had drowned.

When she had married Constantin her insecurity had not helped their relationship, she acknowledged. She had believed she wasn't good enough for him, as she hadn't been good enough for her father. She had never questioned why Constantin hadn't shown any emotion when they had buried Arianna because she had been too wrapped up in her own feelings to care about his, she thought guiltily.

'Oh, my darling, what's wrong?' she whispered, dropping down onto her knees in front of him.

He jerked his head out of his hands and stared at her through red-rimmed eyes. 'Isobel?' He seemed to realise he was not imagining her, and his expression became even more ravaged. 'Why are you here?' He ran his hands through his hair. 'You have to go,' he told her harshly. 'You have to go away from me…and never come back.'

She touched his wet cheek that she had slapped before she had run out of Casa Celeste. 'Why do you want me to leave you?'

'Because…' He gave a ragged groan. 'Because I'm afraid I could hurt you.'

'The only way you could hurt me is if you send me away,' she said with raw honesty. 'When you asked me to wear your ring again yesterday I hoped it was because you wanted our marriage to work. Hearing that you had been forced into a reconciliation by your uncle in order to be appointed Chairman of DSE made me think that you… you didn't care about my feelings. But that's not true, is it?'

She wished he would say something instead of allowing her to blunder on and no doubt make a fool of herself. A memory flashed into her mind of the look of worry and strain on his face when he had rushed back from New York to be with her at the hospital after the stalker had attacked her. 'I think you do care a little,' she said huskily.

Instead of replying, he got to his feet and strode into the en-suite bathroom, emerging moments later rubbing a towel over his face. He seemed more in control of himself, but his chest heaved as if it hurt him to breathe.

'There are things you don't know,' he said abruptly. 'A secret that I have kept since I was seventeen.'

'If our marriage is to stand a chance, we can't have secrets from each other.'

A nerve jumped in Constantin's jaw. 'If I tell you this secret I guarantee you will leave and you'll wish you had never heard the name of De Severino.'

For a moment Isobel felt afraid of what he might reveal in this house of ghosts. Whatever it was clearly haunted Constantin, and he had borne the burden of his secret alone for all of his adult life.

'I think we both have to take that risk,' she said quietly.

He was silent for a few moments—and then, heavily, 'So be it.' He walked over to the window that overlooked the courtyard and stood with his back to her.

'I'm convinced that my father murdered his second wife.'

Shock sent a shiver down Isobel's spine. 'But…I thought Franco loved Lorena.'

'He did love her. He was obsessed with her and he could not bear any other man to look at her.'

'Including you?' Once again, Diane Rivolli's words came into Isobel's mind. *There was something quite cruel about the way Lorena deliberately encouraged Constantin's crush on her, and the way she played father and son off against each other.*

Constantin sighed. 'I was seventeen when my father married again. I returned to Casa Celeste from an all-boys boarding school to find I had a stepmother who was only a few years older than me.

'Lorena's idea of dressing for dinner was to wear a sarong over her bikini,' he said with heavy irony. 'She would flirt with anything in trousers. For a hormone-fuelled, sexually inexperienced teenager she was the ultimate male fantasy.'

'Your father can't have liked you taking an interest in his wife.'

'He hated me spending time with her. There were many rows between me and my father, and my father and Lorena.' He fell silent again, before forcing himself to go on. 'On the day it happened…I had walked into the courtyard and I heard voices from the top of the tower. My father and Lorena were fighting as usual. She was taunting him that he was too old and she told him that she desired *me* more than him.' Constantin grimaced. 'Stupid youth that I was, I actually felt flattered.

'My father was furious. He was shouting at Lorena, and the next minute I saw her topple over the balcony rail, followed seconds later by Franco.'

'I can't imagine how terrible it must have been for you to watch, helplessly,' Isobel murmured.

'I was the only witness,' Constantin said flatly. 'At the inquest I gave evidence that I had seen Lorena fall, and my father had reached out to try and save her but he leaned out too far and also fell. A verdict of accidental death was recorded for both of them.'

'Surely your father was a hero who died attempting to save his wife?'

'That was what everyone believed. I assured myself the events had happened as I had stated. But I'd blocked out much of what happened because I couldn't bear to remember.' Gruesome images flashed into Constantin's mind and he could not repress a shudder. 'There was always something at the back of my mind, something wrong about what I had seen, but I didn't know what bothered me—until the nightmares started.'

He turned his head and glanced at Isobel. 'It was the weekend that I took you to Rome and we became lovers. You were unlike any woman I'd met before, beautiful, innocent, and, as I discovered when I took you to bed, incredibly sensual.' He gave a self-derisive snort. 'I shouldn't have been so pleased that I was your first lover but I felt like a king.'

Isobel swallowed. 'If that's true, why did you dump me the minute we got back to London? You said it had been a fun weekend but that you were not looking for a relationship, and the next thing I heard you had left the London office and disappeared back to Rome.'

Constantin looked away from her hurt expression. 'While we were in Rome I had a horrific nightmare about what had happened to my father and Lorena at Casa Celeste. I saw them standing on the balcony at the top of the tower. At the inquest I'd stated that I had seen Lorena fall and my father reach for her. But in my dream I saw my father reach towards Lorena *before* she fell.

'It was the missing piece of the puzzle that had troubled me for so long. My nightmare showed me what my conscious mind had blocked out. My father hadn't tried to save Lorena. He had *pushed* her from the top of the tower in a fit of jealous rage before he jumped to his death after her.'

'That's awful!' Isobel's words were an instinctive response to Constantin's shocking revelation. 'It seems unbelievable.'

'I wish it was,' he said grimly. 'Unfortunately it's true. My nightmares always show the same sequence of events. My father was responsible for my stepmother's death.'

Isobel's brow creased in a puzzled frown. 'If it *is* true, I appreciate that your father did a terrible thing. But why did your nightmares only start when you met me? Do I look like Lorena, and remind you of her?' Was that why Constantin had been attracted to her when she had been his office assistant? she wondered.

'No, you look nothing like her.'

'Then why was I the catalyst that made you remember what had happened?'

He did not reply, but Isobel could sense the fierce tension emanating from him. 'I believe the nightmares are a warning from my subconscious,' he finally muttered.

Her confusion grew. 'A warning about what?'

'That I might have inherited the manic jealousy which turned my father into a murderer.'

She tried to make sense of his words. 'You're afraid that you might fall in love with someone in the obsessive way that your father loved Lorena?'

Constantin gave a harsh groan. 'Not someone. *You*, Isabella, I love you. And it's for that reason that I am going to divorce you.'

Isobel's heart swooped and dipped as if she were riding a roller coaster. 'You love me?' she said faintly. 'But you admitted earlier that you asked me to come back to you because your uncle had said he would only appoint you as Chairman of DSE if you reconciled your marriage.'

'I had to make you leave because it's the only way I can ensure your safety. You are better off without me in your life. I hadn't anticipated that you would come back,' he said grimly.

He raked his hair back from his brow with an unsteady hand. 'I realised when we became lovers in Rome three years ago that I was in trouble. You got to me in a way no other woman ever had. The nightmare terrified me because I wondered if I could have a jealous streak like my father, so, I backed off and ended our affair.

'When you told me you were pregnant it seemed that fate had played a hand. I told myself it was my duty to marry you, but secretly I was glad of the excuse to continue our relationship.'

'We were happy in those first months of our marriage,'

Isobel remembered. 'But everything changed when we came here, to Casa Celeste.'

'The nightmares started again, but they were worse, because I dreamed that it was you and I at the top of the tower, and I pushed you from the balcony in a jealous rage. I'd never felt possessive of any woman but you,' Constantin said rawly. 'I thought that if I stopped myself from loving you, then you would be safe from my jealousy. But after you had the miscarriage I didn't know how to help you. I couldn't blame you for turning to your friends from the band for support, but I hated the fact that you wanted to be with them rather than me.

'Jealousy is the worst kind of poison. It seeps into your blood and eats away at your soul. When you left me to go on tour with the Stone Ladies it was almost a relief to know that you were no longer in danger from me. You had a new life, a successful career, and I assumed that you and Ryan Fellows were lovers.'

Constantin paused, aware that he had to be totally honest with Isobel. 'I was furious with my uncle for issuing an ultimatum to go back to my marriage. I'd seen you and Fellows on a TV chat show hinting that you were in a relationship. When I kissed you at the party in London I'd intended to persuade you to come back to me purely so that Alonso would make me Chairman.'

Isobel bit her lip. 'So it was all fake? Your kindness, the yellow roses you bought for me?' His tender passion that had given her hope for their marriage, she thought, her heart aching.

'When you were attacked by the stalker, my *only* thought was to protect you. I brought you to Rome and immediately fell under your spell again. But the evening we had dinner at Pepe's forced me to accept that I was still a threat to you.'

'We had a lovely evening,' she said, puzzled. 'I felt safe from the stalker for the first time in months. *You* made me feel safe.'

'The waiter at the restaurant smiled at you and I wanted to rip his head off.' Constantin's jaw clenched. 'I hate other men looking at you.'

'Well, I hate women looking at you. When I saw pictures in the newspapers of you with beautiful women I felt sick with jealousy. It's a normal human emotion,' Isobel said gently.

'My father killed his own wife out of jealousy. You can't tell me that was normal behaviour.' Constantin shook his head. 'I've turned down the role of Chairman of DSE and resigned from my position as CEO. I asked my uncle to meet me here this morning to give him the news, but you spoke to him first, before I'd had a chance to tell him my plans.'

'What are your plans? DSE is more important to you than anything else and I can't believe you've resigned.'

'I have no idea what I'm going to do,' he said listlessly. 'I had thought that if I left the company and Casa Celeste, cut myself off from everything connected to my father, you and I could start a new life together. But last night I had another nightmare, and I realised that I can't hide from my past and I can't change the fact that I am Franco De Severino's son. I inherited my father's jealous streak, and I never want to find out what it might make me capable of.'

He stared at Isobel's beautiful face and visualised his stepmother's broken body at the base of the tower. 'Don't you see, Isabella? I can't risk loving you,' he said harshly. '*For God's sake*, and, more importantly, for *your* sake, leave me and go and get on with your life.'

For a long time after Constantin had heard the bedroom door close behind Isobel, he stood and stared unseeingly down at the courtyard. *It was over.* She now knew that she had married the son of a murderer. She understood that De Severino blood was bad blood, and, unsurprisingly, she had gone.

Raw emotion clogged his throat. If there was a hell, it could not be worse than the place he was in right now. His single consolation was the knowledge that he had done everything he could to protect Isobel. Telling her about his father had made him feel unclean, and, growling a savage imprecation, he stripped out of his clothes and stepped into the shower.

The powerful spray cleansed his body but nothing could wash the darkness from his soul. Memories of Isobel filled his mind; her smile, her honey-gold hair spilling across the pillows, her lips parting beneath his. *Dio*, she had gone, and his life had no purpose. He tilted his head and let the spray run down his face, because that way he could kid himself that they were not tears streaming from his eyes.

The steam from the hot water and the noise of the powerful spray blinded and deafened him, and he was unaware that he was no longer alone until a hand touched his shoulder.

'*Santa Madre!* You nearly gave me a heart attack.' He took the towel Isobel handed him and roughly dried himself, before hitching it around his waist. It was only a hand towel and barely covered his thighs. He saw her eyes flick down his body and felt an inevitable tightening in his loins. 'Why are you still here?' If she did not leave he was afraid he might never let her go. 'If you're worried about driving my car, I'll call a taxi for you.'

'I'm not going anywhere,' Isobel told him calmly. 'I went to the courtyard and looked up at the tower. I'm not sure that you could have seen clearly what took place on the balcony all those years ago.

'You witnessed a terribly traumatic event when you were seventeen,' she said gently. 'I think you felt guilty that you'd had a crush on your stepmother and you heard your father arguing with Lorena about you. Maybe you even felt that Franco had a right to be angry with his flirtatious wife. When you saw Lorena fall you believed that your father might have pushed her in a jealous rage, but you don't really know that he did.'

'My nightmares always show the same thing.' He closed his eyes briefly, haunted by images that sickened him. 'Sometimes in my dreams I see *you* falling from the tower,' he muttered. 'I wake up with my heart pounding with fear because I could not bear for something so terrible to happen to you as happened to Lorena.'

Isobel's heart contracted as she watched his eyes darken with pain. How could she ever have thought that he was emotionless and cold? 'You were deeply traumatised by what you witnessed that day. But, Constantin, even if you *did* see your father push Lorena, it doesn't mean that you have inherited murderous tendencies. You are not Franco, you're you, and from what I've heard about your father you are very different from him.

'We are each of us in charge of our own destinies,' she said fiercely. 'You should be proud of the man you are, and all you have achieved at DSE, as I am proud of you.'

He let out a ragged breath. 'So, are you a psychologist now?'

'No, I'm your wife who loves you with all her heart.' Isobel held his gaze. 'I found this on your desk.' She held up the new divorce petition his lawyer had sent him stating that they had lived apart for two years, and tore it up.

'I am going to remain your wife until death us do part, as we both promised.'

For timeless seconds he said nothing, and fear curdled in her stomach that she had misunderstood him earlier, that he hadn't meant it when he'd said he loved her. But then he moved and hauled her against his big chest.

'Dammit, Isobel, I can't fight you when you don't play fair.'

'Why do you want to fight me?' she said softly.

He took a shuddering breath. 'Because I'm scared of loving you,' he admitted in a low tone that revealed the intensity of his emotions. 'Because I'm scared I'll lose you.'

She thought of the little boy who had been forbidden to cry at his mother's funeral, the man who had been dry-eyed when they had buried their baby daughter but who had created a rose garden in Arianna's memory.

'You won't lose me,' she told him fiercely. 'I will love you for ever.' She cupped his face in her hands and sought his mouth, kissing him with all the love inside her, with her heart and soul, willing him to take the risk and find the happiness she knew belonged to them.

'*Ti amo, Isabella.*' His voice shook. 'I swear I will keep you safe, and I will never hurt you.'

'Then you must promise that you will always love me.'

'Let me show you.' He swept her up into his arms and carried her into the bedroom where he made love to her with such tender passion that she could not hold back her tears. 'Don't cry, *tesorino*,' he said huskily, 'or you'll make me cry too.'

She saw the brightness in his blue eyes, his vulnerability that he no longer tried to hide from her, and her heart overspilled with love for him.

'There will be times when we will smile and laugh, but there'll be other times when we'll cry, because that is the way of life. But we will laugh and cry together. And always we will love each other,' she vowed.

Constantin smiled. 'Always, my love.'

EPILOGUE

Eighteen months later.

THE AUDIENCE AT Wembley Arena were calling for the Stone Ladies to return to the stage. *One more song*, they chanted, but the band had already played three encores and there were groans from the crowd as the lights came on, signalling that the concert was over.

Backstage it was manic as usual. The sound crew were already busy dismantling equipment, the band's manager, Mike Jones, was giving a live TV interview. Someone from the PR team grabbed Isobel and asked her to sign autographs for fans who had backstage passes. She paused to chat to the fans for a couple of minutes before she squeezed through the crowd.

Ryan caught up with her. 'Izzy, do you and Constantin want to come and have a drink with me and Emily?'

'I think we'll go straight home tonight. But the two of you will come to dinner next week with Carly and Ben, won't you? Constantin wants to show you his new car. Honestly, the two of you are like kids when it comes to fast cars,' she said drily.

Ryan grinned. 'We're looking forward to it.'

He disappeared into his dressing room, and Isobel reached the place she wanted to be. 'It's lucky you're taller than everyone else,' she told her husband as he curved his arms around her waist and drew her close. 'It makes you easy to spot in a crowd.'

He dropped a light kiss on her mouth and when she parted her lips he deepened the caress and it became a sensual prelude to the passion that would soon follow. 'It was another fantastic concert, but you must be exhausted after performing on four consecutive nights. It's time I took you and our son home, *tesorino*.'

Isobel felt her insides melt as she looked at the four-month-old baby boy who was tucked securely into the crook of Constantin's arm and was fast asleep. 'How was Theo while I was on stage? Did he settle okay after his feed?'

'He slept through the entire concert.' Constantin laughed. 'The fans obviously love your music but I'm afraid your son isn't impressed that his mother is a rock star.'

She laughed. 'Wait till he's old enough to learn to play the drums.'

'I'm already planning on having the nursery sound-proofed.'

Whittaker was waiting outside to drive them back to Grosvenor Square. Once Theo had been strapped into his baby seat Constantin climbed into the back of the car and Isobel rested her head on his shoulder.

'Home sounds nice,' she said sleepily.

'It won't be long before our new home is finished. I spoke to the architect today, and he says we will be able to move into the villa before Christmas.'

'Theo will spend his first Christmas at Casa Rosa. I can't wait.'

Constantin smiled to himself as he thought of the surprise he had in store for Isobel. She had no idea that he had commissioned a recording studio to be built adjoining the new house. She had understood why he hadn't wanted to live at Casa Celeste, and the four-hundred-year-old house was now a museum managed by a group of historians who were restoring the huge art collection acquired by past generations of the De Severino family.

Casa Rosa was a modern villa, which had been built close to the chapel where their daughter was buried. Constantin had been closely involved with the construction of the home he had helped to design for his wife and son and the children they hoped to have in the future. Although he had withdrawn his resignation from DSE, he had chosen to share the roles of Chairman and CEO with his cousin Maurio, which gave him time to travel to concerts with Isobel and take care of Theo while she was performing.

She lifted her head from his shoulder. 'What are you smiling about?'

'I was just thinking that life is pretty damned perfect.' He stared into her clear hazel eyes and knew that her look of love was reflected in his own gaze. 'I never knew I could be this happy, *mio amore.*'

Isobel looked at her baby son who had arrived in the world without fuss and had helped to heal the ache in her heart. When Theo was old enough they would tell him about his older sister and take him to play in Arianna's rose garden.

She turned back to her husband and caught her breath when she saw the raw emotion revealed in his bright blue eyes. There were no secrets between them now, just a love that would last a lifetime.

'I love you,' she said simply. They were only three little words, but they meant the world.

* * * * *

#3309 TO WEAR HIS RING AGAIN
by Chantelle Shaw

When Isobel sees her husband, Constantin de Severino, again, the temptation to wear his ring once more becomes overwhelming. But as long-dormant secrets are uncovered, Isobel must decide if Constantin is still hers to have and to hold...

#3310 INNOCENT IN HIS DIAMONDS
by Maya Blake

CEO Bastien Heidecker holds Ana Duval's family responsible for the destruction of his own. So he'll satisfy his craving for her, then discard her. But what happens when he discovers that Ana is innocent in *every* sense of the word?

#3311 THE MAN TO BE RECKONED WITH
by Tara Pammi

Even though he's furious that Riya has brought him back to face his past, Nathanial Ramirez can't refuse her bait. Now he'll use every sensual weapon in his considerable arsenal to secure his heritage...and get Riya in his bed!

#3312 CLAIMED BY THE SHEIKH
by Rachael Thomas

Prince Kazim banished his wife from his kingdom long ago but now he needs her back. Amber's always threatened Kazim's tightly held control, yet to save his nation—and his marriage—he must finally make the ultimate claim...on his wife!

YOU CAN FIND MORE INFORMATION ON UPCOMING HARLEQUIN® TITLES, FREE EXCERPTS AND MORE AT WWW.HARLEQUIN.COM.

HPCNM0115RB

REQUEST YOUR FREE BOOKS!

2 FREE NOVELS PLUS
2 FREE GIFTS!

YES! Please send me 2 FREE Harlequin Presents® novels and my 2 FREE gifts (gifts are worth about $10). After receiving them, if I don't wish to receive any more books, I can return the shipping statement marked "cancel." If I don't cancel, I will receive 6 brand-new novels every month and be billed just $4.30 per book in the U.S. or $4.99 per book in Canada. That's a saving of at least 14% off the cover price! It's quite a bargain! Shipping and handling is just 50¢ per book in the U.S. and 75¢ per book in Canada.* I understand that accepting the 2 free books and gifts places me under no obligation to buy anything. I can always return a shipment and cancel at any time. Even if I never buy another book, the two free books and gifts are mine to keep forever.

106/306 HDN FVRK

Name _____ (PLEASE PRINT)

Address _____ Apt. #

City _____ State/Prov. _____ Zip/Postal Code

Signature (if under 18, a parent or guardian must sign)

PRINCESS'S SECRET BABY

* * *

PRINCESS Leila of Surhaddi no longer existed.

The elevator took her down to the reception area and Leila looked around for a moment.

Elegance was the policy at the Harrington and famous people welcomed that they could be there without fuss. Such was her beauty, though, such was her way, that people could not help but look.

She heard the sound of a piano and followed it. As Leila walked into a bar the chink of glasses and the sound of subdued conversation dimmed for a moment. She stood in the doorway in absolute terror, not that she showed it. What the hell had she even been thinking?

But then *it* happened.

Then, for the first time in her entire life, Leila felt welcome when she walked into a room. A man at the bar turned around and his chocolate-brown eyes met hers. For a brief second he startled and then frowned, as if trying to place her, and then he simply smiled.

Leila had never, not once, felt so welcome. His eyes did not roam her body as other men's had; they simply met and held hers. Leila found that she was smiling back. Then, as naturally as breathing, she walked over to him.

"I've changed my mind," the man said. His voice was rich and expensive and he turned and spoke to the barman. "I'll have another drink after all." Then his eyes returned to Leila's. "What can I get you?"

Her whole life she had been afraid, yet she wasn't now.

* * *

*Step into the gilded world of **The Chatsfield**!*
Where secrets and scandal lurk behind every door...

Reserve your room!
March 2015